Joanna Ford had the bluest eyes he'd ever seen!

That was Brett's first thought as he was introduced to her.

"Hi, Joanna, it's nice to meet you."

The hand she extended to him was tentative, but the touch of her palm in his packed a real wallop. "I...hope my being here isn't going to be an inconvenience."

"Absolutely not," Brett replied. If he'd been caught off guard by the contrast between her angelic features and sinful curves, it was nothing compared to the impact her sudden smile had on him.

He was honest enough to admit to himself that, had Joanna been a few years older, his vow to avoid women would have been postponed....

Author's note—For Female Readers Only!

When my editor first asked me if I'd like to write a book entirely from the hero's viewpoint, I jumped at the chance. First, because of the challenge it presented. We all know guys don't think like us—although, let's be honest, the world would be a smarter place if they did!

The second reason was…revenge. Now, as a married woman, the mother of two sons and a romance author, I'm anything but anti-men. In fact, despite all the undue stress they cause us women with their quirky little habits, they are by and large an endearing species.

My great fear, however, has always been that we don't really cause them nearly as many problems as they cause us. They constantly ridicule us for our women's intuition; but really, what can we do when they are so reticent about revealing their true thoughts or feelings to us?

They can, on rare occasions, be perceptive themselves— as was proven when my husband's best mate, Mark, informed me that my husband-to-be was crazy about me…long before he came to that realization himself!

I confess I had a lot of fun "thinking" like a man for this story, and I hope you'll get a few smiles reading it, too.…

Oh, and incidentally, this book is dedicated to my fourteen-year-old son, Jordan, whose quick thinking and instincts for protecting the female sex saved not only two chapters of this book but also his little sister's life when she inadvertently switched off the computer! Ah, men…you gotta love 'em!

Alison Kelly

ALISON KELLY

Man about the House

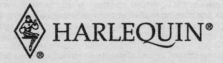

TORONTO • NEW YORK • LONDON
AMSTERDAM • PARIS • SYDNEY • HAMBURG
STOCKHOLM • ATHENS • TOKYO • MILAN • MADRID
PRAGUE • WARSAW • BUDAPEST • AUCKLAND

ISBN 0-373-11975-5

MAN ABOUT THE HOUSE

First North American Publication 1998.

Copyright © 1998 by Alison Kelly.

Printed in U.S.A.

PROLOGUE

THE customs officer who'd welcomed the previous passenger into the country with minimum fuss, despite grubby
jeans, a bare chest and tatty leather waistcoat, was becoming more and more pedantic in his inspections of Brett's
Louis Vuitton luggage. And on the tail-end of a delay
plagued flight from LAX Brett was becoming more and
more anxious to get it over with.

'Fair go, mate,' he said irritably. 'Do I *look* like a sleaze-
bag drug courier?'

'I couldn't say, sir,' the man informed him, his face ex-
pressionless as he flicked his eyes over Brett's crumpled
designer sports coat. 'But the sniffer dogs didn't seem to
think so.'

Despite himself, Brett grinned at the subtle, ironic humour of the man's response. He'd missed the Australian
trait of blending dry, cheeky wit with a perfectly straight
face during the four years he'd been in the 'let's-do-lunch'
capital of the world. The small, unexpected dose of it now
reminded him he'd re-entered the pretention-free zone of
home.

After the hectic pace of his LA existence as producer of
a cable TV lifestyle show, in a business climate that worshipped over-achievers and workaholics, Brett was more
than ready to embrace the more laid-back attitude of his
home country. For all that the television and film industries
in Australia operated on only a fraction of the budgets
available to their North American counterparts, the commitment of those involved seemed more, not less, professional. There was *no* way the star of an Aussie television
series would arrogantly not turn up for work until his salary

was doubled, because there was no way network executives would cop for that kind of prima donna behaviour.

Okay, so coming home meant he was going to be earning less, but conversely he'd be less stressed and in a better position to re-evaluate the current state of his life and what was important to him. Thirty-four seemed like a good age to do this, especially since he'd wasted the last three years of his personal life on a live-in relationship with a former-model-wannabe-TV-presenter who'd cared more about what he could do for her career than she had for him.

He groaned mentally when the image of Toni Tanner popped into his head, vowing that in the wake of the pouty, manipulative, china-smashing shrew he'd stupidly imagined himself in love with the only women he wanted in his immediate future were his twin sister, Meaghan, her daughter, Karessa, and his mother.

When the customs clerk finally cleared his luggage, it was with an easy smile and an uncomplicated, 'Welcome home, mate.'

Maybe it was the accent, but somehow those words sounded a hell of a lot more sincere than all those routine 'have a nice day's he'd been on the receiving end of for the last four years. More than once he'd been tempted to snap back with, Don't tell me what kind of day to have! if only for the sake of seeing if that would generate an honest, impulsive response. Though to be fair, he reasoned, steering his luggage trolley towards the exit, that particular habit hadn't started grating on him until Toni had, and—

'Brett! Hoy, Brett! Over here!'

Turning his head, he immediately spotted the grinning, arm-waving antics of his sister and his fourteen-year-old niece.

CHAPTER ONE

THEY crossed the car park with Karessa chattering nineteen to the dozen, as if it was imperative Brett be brought up to speed with everything that had happened in her life since his visit six months ago at Christmas. One of his fears when he'd made the decision to move overseas was that the easy relationship he'd shared with his niece would become stilted by distance or just the inevitable changes of her moving from childhood to young adulthood. It was a relief to know it hadn't happened, that Karessa could still be as open and spontaneous with him as she'd been at two, eight and ten.

From the day she was born, in the absence of a father or grandfather, Brett had taken it upon himself to provide her with a male role model. Though he hadn't entirely ruled out having his own kids, given his habit of falling for women with zero interest in becoming mothers he suspected his niece was going to be as close as he got to fatherhood. But hearing her gush about various boys and bands made it even more obvious his 'little' niece was rapidly growing up.

In contrast to her mother, who, like him, was a green-eyed blonde, his niece had inherited her late grandfather's russet hair and whisky eyes, but like all the McAlpines she was going to be tall—perhaps taller than her mother. At five foot ten, Meaghan was only six inches shorter than Brett, but already Karessa stood eye to eye with her. Or at least she would if she ever actually stood still instead of leaping about like a hyped-up thoroughbred filly.

'And you know what's *really* cool, Brett? Meggsie said I can work at the agency during the next school break!'

Brett frowned at his sister. 'You're going to start her modelling?'

'*No, I am not.*' The reply was accompanied by a determined look at Karessa. 'What I'm hoping to do is *discourage* such stupidity. So feel free to back me up on this, little brother.'

Brett laughed at the abject plea for him to do just the opposite his niece shot at him. 'Think you guys can at least give me a few days before expecting me to act as Solomon?'

'Take as long as you like,' Karessa said, grinning. 'I'm not going to change my mind, no matter what you say, anyway.'

'Now there's a shock,' he said dryly. 'No need for a DNA test to prove you're Meaghan's daughter.'

Just then the two women came to a halt beside a sparkling red, latest model BMW. There was one thing he hadn't missed while he was away: his sister's thrill-seeker driving style!

'Of course, Karessa,' he said, looking at the very crumpled rear passenger side fender, 'we can always hope you inherited *my* driving skills. Hell, *anyone's* save Demolition Donna's, here.'

'I know,' his niece said solemnly. 'That's my nightly prayer.'

'Oh, shut up, both of you!' Meaghan's rebuke was weakened by the hint of a reluctant smile. '*It wasn't my fault.* I was pulling out of the mall parking lot into traffic and this young idiot slammed into the side of me.'

'Late twenties. Body to die for. Major hunk,' Karessa tossed over her shoulder as she slid into the back seat.

'He was a reckless *idiot*!' her mother insisted.

'Meaghan, if you were pulling into traffic, then *you* were in the wrong,' Brett said mildly, wondering what his chances were of talking his sister into letting him drive. 'Unlock the trunk, will you? So I can load my luggage.'

'You're back in Australia now; it's a *boot*, not a trunk.

And how come if I was in the wrong I wasn't charged, huh?'

'You offered to fix them up with a couple of models?' he teased.

Karessa's grinning face poked through the window. '*He* didn't want to call the cops.'

'Because *he* knew he was in the wrong!' Meaghan retorted. 'Besides, he was driving a four by four with bull bars. There was no damage to his car, so Mum and Joanna talked him into just taking my insurance details.'

Brett closed the boot. 'Joanna?'

'Joanna Ford. She works for the agency.'

Well *that* explained things, he concluded, too easily able to visualise a scene where his sister was loudly and vehemently denying all responsibility while one of the agency's models was batting her baby blues and flaunting her figure in a bid to further confuse the other driver. The poor guy wouldn't have stood a chance.

The sight of his sister moving to the driver's door quickly rerouted his concerns from her last unfortunate victim to trying to avoid meeting another today. 'I'll drive if you like.'

Meaghan looked utterly perplexed by his offer. 'You've spent the last four years in a country where they drive on the wrong side of the road... Why on earth would I want you to drive?'

'Community consciousness?'

'Oh, very droll. For your information this is only my second prang in fourteen months. And *neither* were my fault so just quit the wisecracks and get in the car.'

She shook her head as she slid behind the wheel. 'To think I've been looking forward to having you back, even knowing you'd be looking over my shoulder every day.'

Brett strapped himself into the passenger seat as the engine was gunned to life with more gusto than was necessary or intended by the vehicle's engineers. 'I'm not going to be looking over your shoulder, Meaghan.'

'Oh, sure, that's what you say now... But I *know* you, Brett McAlpine. The only reason you've stayed a silent partner in the agency these last four years is because you've been on another continent. Once you get back in the office you aren't going to be able to help yourself.'

'I'm not going to be back in the office.'

'What?' Meaghan turned fully to look at him, bringing the steering wheel with her.

'Watch out!' he shouted, grabbing for the dashboard.

His sister, typically, remained unperturbed at narrowly missing a signpost. 'What do you mean, you won't be coming into the office? You own half the business.'

'Well, for a start you don't need me.' It was the truth. Meaghan's driving might suck, but she'd proved herself to have a good head for business. 'In the time I've been away you've managed it brilliantly,' he said honestly.

'Aw, but I've been looking forward to working with *you,* Brett,' Karessa whined, pushing her head between the front seats to peer woefully at him. 'I thought you'd let me be your assistant or something. If you're not going to be there I'll probably get stuck doing Meggsie's dumb filing. Or something equally borr-ring.'

'You won't have time for ''dumb filing'', daughter dear,' Meaghan said, looking into the rearview mirror. 'You're going to be too busy sharpening my pencils.' Her eyes flicked to Brett. 'Now, would you care to tell me what brought this on? When you said you were coming home to stay, I assumed we'd be running the business together. That *was* the plan when you left.'

From Brett's side of things it hadn't been so much a plan as an expedient excuse. When he'd suggested he go fifty-fifty in the modelling agency five years ago, it had only been because he knew how desperately Meaghan wanted to buy the business and the precise limits of her finances. Had he merely offered to lend her the money his sister, being the most stubbornly proud person on God's earth, would have refused his help point-blank, so he'd gone with the line that he was looking for something he could 'come back to' when he got bored with television production. He'd had no real desire to run a modelling agency back then, and even less now. The last thing he needed was facing a lot of Toni clones on a daily basis, who'd have no hesitation about fawning over 'the boss' if they thought it would help them get ahead.

'Yeah, well, I've changed my mind. I've had some promising offers from the networks here, and there's another venture I'm mulling over. By the way, has Mum given you any idea when she'll be back?'

Meaghan shook her head. 'You know Mum. But she did say that knowing you'd be here to keep an eye on business for her she'd feel less pressured to hurry back.' She grinned. 'Nice to know she's started transferring the heat to someone else at last.'

The comment confirmed Brett's suspicions that the only reason their semi-retired mother had requested he 'keep an eye on business' while she was overseas was because she still hadn't given up the idea of having one of her children take over the running of her interior design business. Kathleen McAlpine's driving ambition in life had been to establish a "true" family business which she could pass on to her children and grandchildren in due course. However, while her only two children had inherited their mother's tenacity and eye for colour, they lacked her passion for building an interior design dynasty.

Meaghan had started out following their father's career path of fashion design, before falling into modelling for a short while and ultimately joint ownership of the agency with him. Brett, meanwhile, had completed an Arts and Communications degree, lucked into a job as a set designer, then used his good fortune to get a job as a researcher on a current affairs programme. From there, he'd gradually worked his way up to production assistant. His switch from working, quite literally, behind the scenes of current affairs to travel and lifestyle shows had been more a case of accident than planning, but one which allowed him to exercise his communication skills in tandem with his creativity.

He wasn't absolutely certain how long television production would continue to hold his interest, but he did know that when he *was* ready for a career change it wouldn't be in the direction of interior decorating. It wasn't that he doubted he'd be successful at it—he'd inherited both his fashion designer father's eye for clothing and his mother's flair for co-ordinating furnishings—he just couldn't see any challenge or excitement in telling someone what colour to paint their walls or where to hang their Dali print. On the other hand, he'd recently come to the decision that opening a chain of stores selling quality furnishings to the upper and middle income earners had the potential to be a very lucrative investment. It might also be a way of appeasing his mother's disappointment when he told her once and for all he wasn't interested in taking over her busi—

He and Karessa swore in unison as Meaghan jumped on the brakes with whiplash-inducing force. Their driver, however, was blithely unconcerned that she'd almost ran up the backside of the car in front of them—the driver of which had mistakenly assumed Meaghan took note of surrounding traffic and that using his indicator was sufficient notice that he was changing lanes.

'By the way, Brett,' she said calmly, 'you're going to need a car. I've got a friend who owns a BMW dealership who'll do you a good deal if you're interested.'

Considering the number of cars Meaghan had gone through in the last seventeen years, he would have expected her to be on a first-name basis with every car salesman and panelbeater in Sydney. 'Thanks, but I'm not in any rush. I'll use Mum's until I decide what I'm going to—'

'No, you can't.'

'Let me guess,' he groaned. 'You've been exercising it while she's been away and as a result it's gone to the big car dump in the sky.'

'For your information, smarty, it's in A1 condition in her garage! It's just that once Joanna gets her licence, she'll need it to get to work.'

He blinked. 'Who?'

'Joanna Ford—the—'

'Oh, right. The one who helped you out at your last accident scene. Why's she driving Mum's car?'

'Because she doesn't have one and Mum said she could. How else is she going to get to work in the city every day?'

'Well, last time I was here there were these things called buses.'

'Get real, Brett!' Karessa piped from the back seat. 'You know what an uphill hike it is from Nan's place to the nearest bus stop.'

'Nan's place!' He straightened in the seat. 'This Joanna's living at Mum's?'

Meaghan nodded. 'Has been for about two months now.'

Oh, great! Here he'd been, imagining himself mentally and emotionally regrouping in blissful solitude, only to find out his absent mother had a model in residence. A damn *model* of all things!

'Would you mind telling me *why* Mum would find it necessary to bring in a boarder?'

'Don't be ridiculous, Brett! Joanna's not *paying* to live there. Mum only managed to talk her into taking up the offer by telling her she needed a house-sitter while she was away. Of course, back then no one knew *you'd* suddenly decide to come home and need somewhere to stay.'

'Gee, the warm welcome got cold fast. Not long ago you claimed you were looking forward to having me home.'

'I was—I am.' She shrugged off the lack of conviction in her voice. 'It's just it would've been better for everyone if you'd had your own place to go to.'

'Well, I'm not going to disagree there, kiddo,' he said dryly. 'But I could hardly tell Glen I wanted him and Tracy to move out of my place when she's practically one contraction away from giving birth to their fifteenth kid in three years.'

When he'd first decided to head overseas, renting his house to his newly married cousin for the two years he'd originally intended being away had seemed like a smart thing to do. Then, when he'd deluded himself into believing his future was with Toni, he'd extended the arrangement he'd made with Glen for a further three years. His cousin had since begun reproducing at such a rapid rate Brett suspected the guy *had* to be ignorant as to what was causing it, but when a guy had three kids under three and a fourth due any minute you didn't chuck him out in the street.

So, now he was stuck having to share his mother's house until he could make alternative arrangements. Wonderful. 'Exactly how long is this Joanna person going to be staying?'

'As long as she wants to.' His sister's look was sharp.

'You'll really like her,' Karessa assured him. 'Won't he, Mum?'

'Just as long as he doesn't *like* her too much.' There was stiff warning in the statement, but before Brett could say he had no intention of getting tangled up with *any* woman in the immediate future, his sister launched into lecture mode.

'I mean it, Brett,' she said. 'This kid has had a really tough time. When she first came into the agency she had a self-confidence reading of minus one hundred. She's starting to come out of herself a bit now, but she's still emotionally fragile. So if you so much as even think about doing a seduction number on her, I'll personally tear you limb from limb.'

'Trust me, Meaghan, the girl's safe from my unscrupulous claws,' he said facetiously. 'The last thing I need after Toni is another model.'

'She's not a model. Too short. But she's as far removed from that witch Toni as any other human being with a heart.'

Irritated at having his plans disrupted, Brett grunted, wondering how long it would take him to find a decent place to rent. However, his sister and niece were still going on about *Joanna* and how *sweet* she was.

'She's a country girl who came into the agency to enrol in a deportment course right when I was looking to replace our receptionist...' Meaghan was saying, obviously under the misapprehension that he was interested. 'She had no job, next to no money and was staying in a bedsit in inner Sydney—'

'Oh, well, it's easy to see where common sense would advise lashing out on an expensive grooming course in those circumstances,' he said.

'As it happens, Mr Know-It-All, in Joanna's case it was *the* most practical thing she could do! She's an intelligent, ambitious girl, but she had absolutely no—and I mean *zilch*—sophistication. Apparently her parents were well into their forties when she was born, and from what I can gather more Amish than the Amish.'

'Yeah!' his niece endorsed. 'Can you believe she hadn't even seen a CD player until she had to learn how to operate the one at the agency?' Karessa was clearly appalled. 'She was *sooo* embarrassed. And I felt *sooo* sorry for her.'

'What little exposure she had to city life came via a year at some boarding school her older sister dumped her in when their parents passed away,' Meaghan continued. 'Unfortunately, she didn't have any choice but to move back and help her sister run the family business they inherited when she graduated. Apparently it's been passed from one generation to the next since the turn of the century, or something.'

Brett frowned. 'I have a hard time believing the heiress to a well-established family business could be as naive or destitute as you two are making her out to be.'

'You jerk! What are you using for brains?'

It was unclear whether he or the pale-faced cyclist his sister had only narrowly avoided skittling was the intended recipient of her outburst, but before Brett had uncurled his fingers from the dashboard Meaghan had calmly picked up where she'd left off.

'We're talking about a *feed* store here, Brett, not a multinational conglomerate, for heaven's sake. Besides, she couldn't access any of her inheritance until she turned twenty-one. The sister sounds like the Wicked Witch of the West with PMS, but to *really* round off what is the most miserable existence I can imagine, just when poor Joanna thought she'd found true happiness, she discovered the low-life lump of pond scum she was in love with was *married*!'

And *that*, Brett thought, explained precisely why the girl had been taken under the collective wings of his sister and mother.

Meaghan had been only nineteen when she'd got pregnant with Karessa, to a long-time boyfriend who had turned out to be someone else's equally long-time husband. To say she'd been devastated would be a massive understatement. Emotionally she'd come close to having a nervous breakdown as she'd struggled to get past not just the humiliation of having been taken for a fool but her love for a man who'd demanded she have an abortion.

At the time, Brett had been damned lucky not to find himself charged with assault when, reacting to sibling instincts rather than brains, he'd rearranged the guy's very pretty face. And it was probably indicative of his baser, less civilised qualities, but he'd never been able to seriously regret that the mongrel had been killed in an accident before Karessa was born.

'*Brett*! Are you listening to me?'

Meaghan's exasperated tone reefed him from his reverie. 'Huh?'

'I *said*...I want your word you won't put the moves on Joanna.'

She was so intent that if Brett hadn't been amused he might have been angry. 'Sure. You want a signed statement to that effect, or will it suffice if I just swear an oath on the Bible?'

Karessa's laughter from the back seat didn't infect her mother. 'Look, all I'm saying is she's not up to being hit on by you. I know your love 'em and leave 'em style, Brett, and, despite everything she's been through, Joanna's probably still naive enough to fall for it.'

Okay, so *now* he was starting to get angry. 'I'd like to point out that as *debaucherous* as you believe me to be, until a couple of weeks ago I'd been in a monogamous relationship for over *three years*. And that even in the most decadent periods of my lust-infested life I have never found *anything* remotely appealing in gauche, heartbroken country waifs!

'Furthermore,' he added, over his niece's hysterical giggles, 'I currently have about as much interest in getting entangled with another female as I do in being castrated. So your precious receptionist has nothing to fear from me. *Satisfied?*'

Wearing a serene smile, and with no respect for the notorious left-hand bend she was taking, his sister reached across and patted his shoulder. 'Thank you, darling. I knew I could count on you.'

CHAPTER TWO

JOANNA FORD had the bluest eyes he'd ever seen! was Brett's first thought as his niece executed a rapid-fire introduction of him in the foyer of his mother's house. His second was that at about five-seven she might be too short to be a model, but she was also as far removed from his image of a country waif as the climate in the South Pole was from that of the Equator! No wonder the guy Meaghan had collided with had been swayed from calling the cops; Joanna Ford had the looks and body to convince a guy *breathing* wasn't in his best interests!

Her naturally almond-shaped eyes were played up with skilfully smudged eyeliner and long thick lashes that were as dark as the silky jet hair falling over her shoulders. High cheekbones were enhanced to create a dramatic shadow on skin as pale and smooth as alabaster porcelain, and as if to balance the dramatic vividness of her eyes in such a serene face her slightly parted mouth was glossed a slick burgundy. Intriguingly, though, the professional use of cosmetics didn't overpower the essential, almost angelic innocence in the girl's face. Although, Brett thought dryly, he doubted innocence was the look she'd been trying to achieve when she'd dressed.

High, firm breasts were emphasised by a body-hugging black sweater and a waist Brett figured he could have encircled with both hands. The black skirt riding on her hips *might* have been fractionally longer than the belt adorning it was wide, but he couldn't swear it because his eyes were too quickly distracted by the black nylon-encased thighs it displayed before he could do a more thorough visual calculation. Being a legs man, by rights his natural curiosity to check out what lay below the over-the-knee boots she wore meant Brett shouldn't have found them as sexy as he did, but *whoa!* They sure blew his perceived image of a wholesome country girl in blue jeans and Blundstones to smithereens!

The four-inch heels had him scaling down his earlier estimate of her height to about five-three in bare feet, but if she was typical of rural Australia these days he was going to have to give serious consideration to getting into agriculture. A warning glance from Meaghan had him schooling his appreciation into a polite smile.

'Hi, Joanna, it's nice to meet you. Meaghan and Karessa have told me a lot about you.' *Course, not as much as they* didn't *tell me*, he mentally added.

'Oh! Well… I… Er…that is, it's nice to meet you too, Mr McAlpine,' she stammered, blushing furiously as Karessa roared with laughter.

'*Mr McAlpine!* Oh, God, you make him sound as old as Mum!'

'That's because he *is*,' Meaghan retorted. 'And thirty-four isn't *that* old, young lady; it just means nobody can *ground* us.'

Brett could have added that if he was so damned old how come his hormones were acting as if they'd regressed twenty years? But it seemed kinder to put the obviously uncomfortable Joanna at ease. Despite the high fashion make-up and clothes, the way she was twisting her fingers and chewing her bottom lip suggested that in the poise and sophistication stakes even fourteen-year-old Karessa would give her a run for her money.

'Meaghan's a terrible liar,' he said, winking. 'I'm actually four minutes younger than she is, so Karessa's right— you can drop the ''mister'' and just make it Brett.'

The hand she extended to him was tentative, but the touch of her palm in his packed a real wallop.

'I…hope my being here isn't going to be an inconvenience. If it is just say so and I'll move—'

'Joanna, you're *not* going to inconvenience anyone,' Meaghan inserted, her tone dragging his eyes away from the blue ones which had been mesmerising him. *'Is she, Brett?'* One eyebrow arched as she subtly flicked her gaze to his hand, which was still engulfing Joanna's more fragile one.

Instantly he ended the handshake. 'Absolutely not. This house is plenty big enough for both of us, Joanna. Meaghan and I grew up here, and sometimes our paths wouldn't cross for—oh…a week at a time. Even when I wasn't trying to avoid her.'

If he'd been caught off guard by the contrast between her angelic features and sinful curves, it was nothing compared to the impact her sudden smile had on him. The parting of her cupid-bow mouth to reveal perfect white teeth and tiny dimples caused his lungs to seize mid-breath.

'Thank you,' she said. 'I'll try not to cause you too much bother.' The smile was turned up another fifty or so watts before she glanced at Meaghan. 'Meggsie…'

Her use of Karessa's pet name for Meaghan further emphasised her youthfulness, and Brett found himself as irritated as he was grateful for the fact. He was honest enough to admit to himself that had Joanna been a few years older his vow to avoid women would have been postponed.

'Meaghan, if you want to cancel our driving lesson to spend time with your brother, I'll understand. You must have a lot to catch up on. And—'

'Don't be silly! We've loads of time. But c'mon through to the kitchen; I could use a cup of coffee before we go.'

His sister was already on her way from the room when she tossed over her shoulder, 'I'd help you bring your luggage in, Brett, but I'm *too old*. But my darling Karessa will gladly help her *equally decrepit* old uncle.'

Though she tossed a teasing smirk at her daughter as she guided Joanna from the foyer, Brett wryly acknowledged the remark was designed to further reinforce the age difference between him and Joanna. Geez, with a sister like

Meaghan around a guy could actually end up believing he *was* a sleaze!

'C'mon,' Karessa tugged his arm. 'Let's get the stuff in before they scoff down all the cake Mum bought.'

Brett laughed. 'Cute ploy, sweetheart, but I can read you like a book.' Smiling, he fished a small package out of his pocket, tossed it to her, then staggered as she threw her arms around his neck and kissed his cheek.

The wrapping was dispensed with in the same excited haste and enthusiasm Karessa always showed for the gifts he brought her whenever he returned from long trips. And, as always, Brett marvelled that her eyes could still light up with the same genuine wonder and delight they'd had when she'd been a toddler.

'Oh, Brett, I love it!' She pushed the beaten silver bangle onto her left wrist and waved her arm around, admiring it. 'It's almost exactly like yours!'

The moment he saw the stones set in the silver, he suddenly had a colour for those eyes: *turquoise*. Joanna Ford's big, beautiful eyes were the purest of turquoise.

'Oh, thank you so much!' Karessa almost choked him with gratitude. 'Thank you, thank you, thank you!'

He laughed. 'You're welcome. You're welcome. You're welcome!'

'Oh, Brett, I've just gotta go show Mum and Joanna now. Then I'll come right out and help with the luggage, okay?'

'Don't bother; I can handle it,' he told her already departing form. 'Er, by the way, Karessa…is Meaghan really giving her driving lessons?'

'Mmm. Scary thought, huh?'

'You're not wrong, kiddo,' he murmured, although the idea of Joanna Ford's unique beauty being put at even the slightest risk struck him as more criminal than scary.

It took Brett the better part of three days to shake off his jet lag, during which time he saw Joanna a corresponding number of occasions. Once when he'd been crossing the foyer, en route to the living area of the house from his bedroom, and she'd barrelled into him at around a hundred 'k's an hour.

Automatically his hands had gone to her shoulders to steady her, and in the ensuing few seconds she'd simply stood there looking slightly dazed as she stared up at him. Again, on the surface she'd been glamour personified, but in the depths of her turquoise eyes—oh, yeah, turquoise was their precise colour—he'd seen an ocean of uncertainty. In the next instant she'd pushed him away and started muttering an embarrassed apology, explaining she was hurrying to catch the bus to the North Sydney office.

'Hey, if you wait till I pull on a shirt I'll drive you down to the bus stop.' His offer had met momentary wide-eyed confusion, a blush, then a vigorously shaking dark head and a hasty, 'No, er, thanks. I'm fine. I...I'm in a hurry. Bye!'

She'd been out of the front door and had it closed behind her before her perfume could catch up with her. He'd liked her perfume... However, on the second occasion he'd seen her he'd been too far away to smell it.

He'd been on his way out for an evening run just as she'd been climbing into a five-year-old Porsche. Having spent all afternoon in his mother's study, reviewing various job offers, Brett hadn't heard her come in from work and had assumed that, it being Friday night, she'd be late home. People who lived on the upper end of the northern Sydney peninsula didn't usually come all the way home from the city to get changed before going out. Brett had figured the male driver was merely a friend, because if he was a date he'd surely have got out of the car to open the door for her! Plus, she'd been wearing snug-fitting jeans and a bomber jacket, which also pretty much ruled out a romantic dinner at a restaurant.

The third time his and Joanna's paths crossed had been some five hours later, just ten minutes ago, when he'd gone out to check what was causing the security sensor light in the front yard to turn on and off every few minutes. He'd expected to find a neighbour's dog had got out, instead he'd found her, bent over in drizzling rain and heaving her heart out in his mother's azalea bed.

She was a wet, tearful and woebegone sight, and he couldn't do much besides offering her physical support by way of an arm across her shoulders, and emotional support that amounted to verbal assurances that she *would* live and that everything was going to be all right. Which was pretty much what he'd told Meaghan the first time she'd written herself off—and what old Mr Parsons who'd used to live next door had told *him* when as a seventeen-year-old he'd been in exactly the same position Joanna was now. No doubt about it, over the years this particular plant had received a more bizarre fertilising compound than any of the others in the McAlpine family garden.

He didn't know what events had led up to Joanna being in this less than sparkling state of health; there was no sign of her Porsche-driving escort and she wasn't making much sense.

'I...I's not dunk,' she continued insisting as he carried her into the house. 'Don't dink. S'never dink.'

'Well, then, princess, I guess you must be having an allergic reaction to that Jack Daniel's you wear as perfume, 'cause it's sure as hell making my eyes water.'

She frowned up at him. 'Jack? Hoosh Jack?'

'Someone you weren't ready to take on, that's for sure.'

Despite the limpness of her body she was light as a feather, and for an instant Brett considered carrying her down the hall to the bathroom and shoving her under a shower fully clothed. It wasn't as if she wasn't already half drenched and in need of warming up, but she was snuggled against him in such a damn trusting way he couldn't bring himself to do it. Instead, he stopped at the bedroom door and bent his knees so he could open the door without dropping her in the process; the handle, though, gave a useless half-turn, indicating it was locked.

'*Hell.*' He sighed heavily and felt the echo of a softer

one as the body in his arms nestled closer. Even smelling like a brewery, with her long black hair a damp tangle and black tear-tracks streaking her face, she possessed an ethereal beauty that inspired protective instincts only Karessa had previously managed to provoke. If he could get her into her room and convince her to get out of her wet clothes and have a shower, she'd be in good enough shape for him to leave her and let her sleep it off.

'Joanna… Joanna, I'm going to put you down and—'

Her arms tightened around his neck. 'No. Shleep…I'm ashleep.'

'No, you're not, honey,' he said, fighting laughter and the stranglehold she had on him. 'You're what's commonly known as tanked to the gills.'

'Fank oooo,' she mumbled. 'You…nice.'

Shaking his head at her inebriated agreeability, he used his left arm to haul her tighter against his chest for stability while his right forearm supported her lower body in such a way that his hand was free to blindly grab the door handle. His height, the bundle in his arms and the low position of the handle made it something of a juggling act, but fortunately long familiarity with the intricate lock mechanism worked in his favour.

He nudged the door wide with his foot, then used his elbow to flick the light switch on the architrave. Immediately the woman in his arms gave a yelp, and buried her face into his shoulder.

'Sorry, but if you think that's bad, waking up tomorrow is going to feel like you're staring directly into the sun.' He stood for a moment, scanning the room, and decided he could do without emptying the assorted stuffed animals from the wicker chaise in the corner, which meant the bed was the only other place to put her.

Crossing to the broderie anglaise-covered bed, he lowered her to her feet, intending to pull back the comforter. But before he could act on the thought she emitted a delighted whimper and lurched towards it so fast she nearly pulled him down onto it too. He managed to brace himself on the bedhead, and when her arms could no longer maintain the effort of stretching up around his neck, she slumped back onto the mattress.

And this had seemed like a two-second rescue job when he'd started it!

He shook her shoulder. 'C'mon, Joanna, your clothes are wet. You can't go to sleep in them.'

'Yesh…shleep. I wanna go…shleep.'

'Yeah, I'm sure you do. But you have to change into something else first.'

She pushed him away when he endeavoured to sit her up. '*Shleep,*' she mumbled, rolling sideways to embrace the pillow on the other side of the bed.

'Damn,' he breathed. Trying to coax her into compliance would be a waste of breath, since neither her current comprehension or co-ordination gave him a hope in hell of success. Which meant he either had to let her sleep in clothes that were wet and grubby enough to support incineration over washing or…undress her himself. If Meaghan hadn't been going away for the weekend he'd have taken great delight in calling at—he glanced at his watch—twenty to one in the morning and asking if the 'hands off' instruction she'd issued about his housemate extended to the point of letting her risk pneumonia.

Looking down at the motionless, bedraggled form on the bed, he resigned himself to the fact he couldn't in good conscience just leave her as she was, but dealing with the situation wasn't going to be easy.

Toni had always insisted that a pair of jeans didn't fit right unless you had to lie down on a bed to get into them and then use a coat hanger hook to zip them up. Apparently Joanna adhered to the same fashion philosophy, because had the jeans she was wearing hugged her any tighter they'd have cut off her circulation. Dry, they'd have been tough enough to get off; damp, they were going to be a nightmare. Although executing that particular task was going to be a whole lot easier on his nerves than ridding her of the Lycra knit bodysuit she wore under them, because *that* was more than wet and tight enough to tell him she was *sans* bra.

Damn.

He raked his hair in frustration, then grabbed her boot-shod foot and gave it a hard shake. 'Hoy! Joanna! C'mon, wake up!'

No response. He repeated the action, this time with more vigour and a raised voice. 'Hoy! Wake up!'

The futility of the exercise didn't take long to register. The next time Brett grabbed her ankle it was to start unlacing the trendy pseudo-army boots she wore. If his putting her to bed meant Joanna would suffer severe embarrassment as well as a terminal hangover in the morning…well, damn it, she had no one to blame but herself for getting into this state in the first place!

CHAPTER THREE

BRETT climbed the steep stone steps rising from the beach to the grassed area that his mother always referred to as 'the backyard'. It was, in fact, only a small patch of painstakingly laid and maintained lawn which people failed to notice because it was overwhelmed by the sweeping Pacific view beyond it. For Brett it was the pristine sand and thick rolling waves of Whale Beach which had been his true backyard growing up. There'd only been a handful of days from the time he was ten until he was nineteen that he hadn't felt the urge to grab his board for a quick surf even if the waves weren't ideal.

Today, having woken to discover a surf breaking to near perfection thanks to a pre-dawn storm, the fact he was thirty-four and it was smack in the middle of winter hadn't mattered a whit. Of course, after about twenty minutes, when the initial adrenalin rush of making a ride all the way to the beach on his first choice of wave had worn off, cold and old age had started to prove a diabolical combination. Not *his* age, of course, but the wetsuit he'd fished out of his wardrobe was about thirteen years old; as insulation it was as useful as a screen door on a submarine.

He laughed aloud when he caught himself giving his most beloved tri-fin an affectionate pat as he leaned it against the wall of the laundry, yet in that instant he knew that even though he'd come to no firm decisions about his professional future he'd made the right personal one in coming home. He'd missed this…really missed it. Oh, sure, he could've surfed in California, and on occasion he had, but somehow it suddenly seemed more natural, indeed *es-*

sential that the rest of his life be spent seeing the sun rising over the Pacific rather than setting on it.

Reaching behind his neck, he snared the plaited tail of the wetsuit's zip and was tugging it down when a startled yelp behind him caused him to almost leap free of the clinging latex.

'Lord, Joanna! You frightened the life out of me.' His heart was still beating out of whack. 'You always sneak up on people like that?'

'I... I...I'm sorry. I didn't realise you were home.' She was hugging a pile of bedding and looking everywhere but at him. 'I...er...just wanted to use the washing machine. But it's okay. It can wait. I'll do it later.'

When she went to dart from the room, Brett snagged her arm. 'Whoa, there. Contrary to whatever stories you've heard, I *don't* bite.'

Though she stilled, her head was downcast, and he used his free hand to tilt it. The minute their eyes made contact she flushed the most vivid red Brett had ever seen and he couldn't help smiling. 'Now your skin matches the red lines in your eyes.'

If possible she turned even redder. With the exception of last night, when she'd been totally plastered, whenever she was around him Joanna Ford acted as if she was being asked to deal with an alien. It put an irritating dent in his ego, since women usually made no secret of the fact they enjoyed his attention.

'So, how are you feeling this morning?' he asked. 'And if you say anything but ''half-dead'', I'm not going to believe it.'

Her tongue came out to graze her lip a split second before she spoke, so mesmerising Brett that it took him several seconds to realise he hadn't heard her response. Releasing her chin, he shook his head to clear it. 'Sorry...what?'

The sigh she gave was so heavy he regarded it a disguised blessing she was still hugging the laundry.

Considering his lower body was clad in a wetsuit, the less he was reminded of the fact she even *had* breasts the better off he'd be!

She'd been out cold when he'd finally summoned the courage to strip her wet top from her last night, but, as swift and circumspect as he'd endeavoured to be in averting his gaze, images of their translucent white firmness and cherry-red peaks had tormented him for the better part of the night.

'I said...I'm mortified about what happened last night.'

Her voice was slightly shaky and her knuckles whitened as she tightened her grip on the wad of bedding. She swallowed hard before continuing, 'I don't remember much, except being sick and you talking to me, then helping me inside. I'm sorry you had to find me like that... I know how...how revolting it is to see someone vomit, and I want you to know I appreciate you staying with me and taking care of me.'

It irked the hell out of him that while the tone of her apology was polite and sincere she'd delivered it without once looking at him. He didn't know if she realised he'd been the one to undress her, but suspected she didn't; her embarrassment didn't seem *that* extreme.

'Listen, Joanna, I realise getting drunk and pulling a hangover can blur the brain a bit, but it wasn't the *washing machine* who carried you inside and tucked you into bed.' His bored tone had her head swinging around to him and her mouth opening and closing like a beached fish.

Eventually she managed a sound. A loud, indignant sound. *'I was not drunk!'* The declaration was immediately followed by a painful grimace that called her a liar.

'Sweetheart,' he said through a chuckle, 'if they took blood from you now, they could sell it as eighty proof.'

'I tell you, *I don't drink*. I didn't have anything last night but punch and cola.'

'Uh-huh.' He didn't bother to hide either his scepticism or amusement at her straight-faced avowal. 'And I suppose you *don't* have a hangover this morning either, even though you look like death warmed up.'

'Having *never* been drunk, I don't have the slightest idea what a hangover is,' she told him, devoid of all trace of the previous shyness she'd exhibited around him. 'And if I look a bit off colour it's because I'm obviously coming down with some kind of flu.'

She was absolutely serious, Brett realised. She truly believed she was feeling the way she did because she was getting a bug. Meaghan had said she was naive, but *this*... Hell, it was criminal to let someone as innocent as Joanna Ford out alone!

'The flu, huh?' he said casually. 'Running a temperature?'

'No, but I think the aspirin I took earlier is keeping it at bay.'

'And the aspirin was for...let me guess...that mild headache you have?'

'There's nothing *mild* about it. It feels like—'

'Like your skull is being split in two from the inside?' he inserted, knowingly. 'Except, of course, when a raised voice, a slammed door or even a sneeze makes it seem like someone is using a jackhammer to clear your sinuses.'

Thick black lashes blinked over surprised turquoise eyes. 'Well, yes...I guess that's one way of putting it,' she conceded, her tone tinged with the same hint of doubt that was beginning to show in her wan-looking face.

Brett gave a sage nod and went on. 'And I'd say the odds would be in the red that, despite the fact you've probably brushed your teeth three or four times now, your mouth still feels like it's coated with old cotton wool that's been dipped in vinegar and rolled in sand. Oh, and your stomach probably feels like it's going to cave in too, but the mere thought of actually introducing food to it makes it start recoiling in dread.'

He raised an eyebrow at her ever-increasing frown. 'How's Dr Brett's description of your symptoms so far?

Ah, yes...and shaking your head hurts,' he added, seeing her grimace after doing so.

'Well?' he prodded.

'That's what a hangover feels like?'

'Yep, 'fraid so.' As concern battled with confusion for dominance in her pretty face Brett wished he'd been a little less smug. "I know it's small consolation right now,' he said, 'but you aren't the first person to have one, Joanna.'

'But my stomach doesn't feel like you said,' she told him, in a grasping-at-straws tone.

'Ahh,' he said sagely. 'Then you're obviously what I call a cast-iron gut drunk,' he told her, softening the description with a smile. 'The majority of hangover victims, myself included, cannot look at anything even remotely greasy the morning after. But there's a second category who swear ingesting as much cholesterol-laden food as quickly as possible restores them to a reasonable facsimile of health.' He grinned. 'My bet is you're in the latter category and that you're craving...oh, say, a big plate of bacon and eggs? Or maybe a nice, thick juicy hamburger?'

He allowed himself a smug chuckle as her expression came close to a drool. 'Tell you what, you put those sheets in the machine while I go get dressed, then meet me in the kitchen.'

'Why?'

'Because it just so happens I'm the cure for your hangover,' he said, returning to the task of peeling off his wetsuit. 'I happen to cook the best damned bacon and eggs you'll ever taste.'

'You can't do that while I'm here!' The adamant declaration surprised him.

'Don't be ridiculous. I don't expect you to do all the cooking.'

'I mean you can't just take your clothes off like that!'

'Take my—'

There was no containing his amusement once he'd caught on to where she was coming from, but he sobered quickly when she dumped the bedding onto the floor and pivoted towards the door. Acting purely on instinct, he threw out an arm, barring her escape; he instantly regretted the action when fear flared in those gorgeous eyes.

'It's okay, Joanna,' he said hurriedly. 'I'm dressed. That is, I've got a pair of swimmers underneath.' Once again she flushed pink.

A week ago he'd have sworn blushing had been entirely bred out of the last few generations of females, but Joanna Ford was a real revelation. A very attractive, very sexy revelation. It was clear she didn't know what to say or where to look. Or rather, she was working hard to look at everything bar his bare chest, to which she was currently close enough for him to feel the warmth of her stuttered, 'Oh. Well... I...'

The husky quality of her uncertain whisper sparked interest in muscles of Brett's body which in the wake of the emotional workout Toni had given him weren't supposed to be looking for exercise. They especially weren't supposed to be motivated by a petite twenty-two-year-old with more curves than common sense and a way of nibbling her mouth that made a man want to say, *Hey...taste mine.*

When she did eventually bring her gaze to his face, her demeanour of shy expectation as she slowly slipped a strand of silky jet hair behind her ear almost made him groan. Had any other woman looked at him like that he'd have read it as a come on and accepted the invitation. Hell, he wanted to accept it *now*! Trouble was, as difficult as it was to believe, he doubted Joanna had a clue about the signals she was emitting.

Deciding they both needed space Brett lowered his arm and stepped back. Producing what he hoped was a reassuring smile, he excused himself and headed to the bathroom.

Brett heard her enter the kitchen scant seconds before a soft, awed voice officially announced her. 'You really can cook.'

'You seem surprised.' He spared her a quick glance. 'Can't you?'

'Can't I what?'

'Cook.'

Her laugh was incredulous. 'Of course I can. I've just never met a man who could.'

'Then you must've met a lot of useless, skinny, hungry men.' His teasing comment limped into an awkward silence.

The way she was fidgeting with the carton of eggs lying on the benchtop hinted at her still being uncomfortable in his presence, for which Brett was grateful. It meant she'd be too distracted to notice any semblance of unease he might display, because there was no denying this girl seriously raised the level of his awareness meter. In the half-hour or so since their earlier encounter, she'd donned make-up and a trendy trouser suit and it irritated him. To his way of thinking, the sexy fashion-plate image constituted false advertising by promising things that were way out of this kid's league and strictly off limits to him. *Sans* make-up, dressed in the blue jeans and sweatshirt of earlier, she'd been less of a threat to his good intentions by at least *looking* as innocent and unworldly as she so obviously was. Now she looked as if she not only knew the score but wanted the role of captain-coach in the game.

He tried hard to concentrate on what he was doing, but was so aware of her watching his every move her gaze was almost like a physical touch.

'Um, would you like me to set the table?' she offered, after several minutes of razor-sharp silence which Brett figured *had* to have made her as uncomfortable as him.

'Sure. Thanks.'

Instantly she started into action, moving with the familiarity of having lived in the house for two months.

The kitchen was by no means small, but somehow Joanna's aura managed to fill every atom of space. Brett had never been so aware of another person's presence in his entire life. On two occasions they got in each other's way, and brushing against her felt like being zapped by a current of electricity. But her movements between the cupboards and the table, the sink and the fridge were a distraction even when she wasn't in his line of vision or within touching distance. Bit by bit the musky scent of her perfume won dominance over the aroma of the cooking breakfast, and his heartbeat drowned out the sizzle of the bacon.

The relief when he could finally sit down and have the width of the breakfast table between them was enormous. Well, it was until the silence again became a stilted roar. They might have both been going through the motions of eating with the automation of two robots oblivious to the other's presence, but Brett figured between them they'd exercised more covert glances than a CIA agent did in a career. This was getting ridiculous! He was thirty-four, for God's sake, not fifteen!

'So,' he said, quickly lowering his unintentionally loud voice when she physically started, 'are you feeling any better now you've eaten?'

Nodding, she quickly swallowed. 'A bit.' A tiny smile tugged at her mouth. 'You were right; you are a good cook.'

'I did warn you.'

His teasing didn't draw more than another small smile, but its briefness didn't dull its impact. Brett scrambled to keep the conversation going. 'You like Thai food?'

'I don't know. I've never had it. I had Italian once.'

'Once?'

'My family didn't eat fancy stuff.'

'Well, then, I guess I'll have to introduce you to a wider culinary range while you're here.'

'Oh, no! Really. I wouldn't feel right letting you fix meals for me.'

'Why not? You have to eat, and it's no fun just cooking for myself.'

For several seconds she seemed nonplussed by his logic,

then produced another of those killer smiles. 'All right, but only if we take turns. You cook one meal, I'll cook the next.'

'Fair enough.'

Their gazes met and held, and Brett had a difficult time convincing his libido that he really wasn't interested in any woman right now—much less the young girl across the table. Even if she was the most incredibly beautiful female he'd ever seen. Yet the hypnotic effect of those turquoise eyes made it impossible for him to look away, and they suffused his body with an inner warmth that was as tranquil as it was disturbing.

It wasn't until she lowered her lashes and rose from her chair that Brett was capable of blinking and breathing again.

'Would you like tea or coffee?' she asked.

Caught up in trying to unravel his bemused thoughts, he had to rerun her words twice before they made sense. 'Whatever you're having is fine.'

'I only drink tea,' she told him. 'But I don't mind making you coffee if that's what you want.' The curve of her mouth was almost as bewitching as those of the body she leaned gracefully against the counter, and the item which sprang to the top of his immediate 'want list' wasn't anything as innocuous as either beverage. He managed to bite back the admission. 'Thanks, but tea's okay with me.'

'How do you have it?'

Brett found himself actually having to *think* before making what should have been an automatic response. 'White. No sugar.'

'Darjeeling, Earl Grey or Irish Breakfast?'

It was then his trouble alarm started *clanging*!

The truth was he had no damn interest in what sort of tea he drank and way too much in the woman making it; all of it sexual.

The problem was he wasn't supposed to be in the market for sex. Even more disturbing than discovering he *was*, was finding himself window shopping in an area outside his habitual interest zone.

Which, of course, was Meaghan's fault! he thought testily. *She* was the one who'd placed him in Joanna Ford's proximity. It was bad enough she'd exposed him to the ethereal raven-haired witch currently holding up boxes of tea like a quiz show hostess, but if his sister hadn't erected neon 'keep off the grass' signs around Joanna, he probably wouldn't have given the girl a second glance. After all, as attractive and sexy as she was, it didn't alter the fact she was only eight years older than his niece and *twelve years younger* than him.

What was more, he decided, she was only proving a distraction because he was *allowing* her to be one. Determined to correct that situation right now, he responded to her repeated query about the tea with an uninterested, 'Surprise me,' then stoically refocused his attention on finishing his breakfast. His only reaction to the steaming mug which moments later was placed near his right hand was a head-bent murmur of, 'Thanks.'

Ruing the absence of a newspaper to bury his head in, Brett continued to eat and to drink his tea without once letting his gaze shift beyond the centre of the table. With the passing of each loud, silence-breaking tick of the wall clock he congratulated himself on having triumphed over the temptation to look at his breakfast companion. See? It *wasn't* hard. He could be as indifferent to Joanna Ford and her seemingly mystical intrigue as he could the salt and pepper shaker her long, elegant fingers were idly tracing with slow, sensuous strokes.

'Brett…'

The husky utterance of his name was his undoing, immediately snapping his gaze up to hers.

'I wasn't lying when I said I didn't drink last night,' she told him. 'But I think you're right about me having a hangover.'

A curt nod would have communicated his lack of interest

in further discussion on the subject, but instead Brett heard himself say, 'A contradictory comment, but I take it as meaning you think it's possible you were slipped a mickey.'

Her brow wrinkled. 'Slipped a mickey?' The confused shake she gave her head set her dark hair glittering in the sunlight. 'What does that mean?'

Aw, hell! There ought to be laws against women this unworldly being allowed within a thousand-kilometre radius of a major city. Especially one with a male population. Deciding the sooner Joanna had her beautiful but innocent eyes opened and developed a cynical edge the safer every red-blooded man she was likely to encounter would be, he went on to explain what a Mickey Finn was, concluding with, 'Some idiot with a juvenile sense of humour probably spiked the punch.'

'But mostly I drank cola.'

'Out of a can or bottle?'

She stiffened in her chair and glared at him. 'Look, I mightn't be all that terribly chic and sophisticated...' hearing anger in her voice startled him '...but I *do* know it's good manners to use a glass!'

Prudence had him swallowing the smile trying to force itself from his lips. 'While that social nicety has its place, Joanna, sometimes good manners have to take second place to good sense.

'So,' he said, 'I'll tell you exactly what my father told Meaghan and me when we were sixteen and just starting to hit the party circuit. One: never accept a drink from anyone at a party unless the bottle cap or ring tab is still sealed. Two: never leave a drink somewhere and then go back and drink it later. And three: avoid punchbowls at all costs.

'As Dad used to say, "The most innocuous thing someone will spike a drink with is alcohol, which can leave you sick as a dog. Other things can leave you dead."'

'You mean some people might put *drugs* in someone else's drink?'

'No… Some people *do*.'

At her look of alarm, he hastened to reassure her. 'Relax, Joanna; you might've been plastered last night, but you didn't appear doped.' But then, because she still looked so shocked, concern caused him to add, 'Well, at least I didn't think you did. You don't think you *were*, do you?'

'How would *I* know?' she demanded. 'Until this morning I didn't know I was *drunk*.'

'Good point!' He laughed. 'Well, you'll know next time.'

'There's not going to be a next time,' she told him. 'If I ever have to feel this ill again I want it to be because I'm dead.'

The droll retort indicated Joanna had a sense of humour, which wasn't good. Because after three years of Toni's pouts and petulance, a woman with a sense of humour was all too appealing, especially when she came gift-wrapped with sexy curves and wide-eyed innocence that practically begged to be educated.

Once again enmeshed with his own worrying thoughts, it took him several seconds to notice Joanna had already cleared the dirty dishes and was running water into the sink.

'Don't bother washing them,' he told her. 'Just rinse them and shove them in the dishwasher.'

'I don't mind doing them. I enjoy standing here and looking out at the beach.'

'Yeah? Gee, Meaghan and I always thought it was more fun being *on* the beach, which is why Mum got the dishwasher in the first place.'

'True.' She sent him another of her breath-defying grins. 'But, since I never saw a beach until I was sixteen, I don't consider having to look at one from this distance any real hardship.'

Brett knew his curiosity showed, but rather than voice it he merely crossed to the kitchen linen cupboard and, pulling out a dishtowel, joined her at the sink.

'It's so incredibly beautiful. It must have been wonderful growing up here?'

Though she phrased the words as a question, her attention was fixed firmly on the other side of the ceiling-reaching window, and her enraptured expression as she surveyed the surrounding cliffs, crags, sand and surf suggested she'd merely been uttering her thoughts aloud. Clearly she was in awe of all that lay between them and the horizon.

It was, he supposed, only natural that growing up here had bred a familiarity which to a degree had immunised him against the natural beauty the scene presented, but for some reason Joanna's reaction to it urged him to look back and try to see it through less jaded eyes. When he did it was as if each new wave that rolled in and collapsed on the beach carried a precious but too long ignored memory of the past.

His father teaching him and Meaghan to swim. The Christmas he'd been given his first surfboard and had been practically tied to a chair to get him to stay out of the water long enough to eat dinner with the multitude of relatives who'd turned up for a hot turkey dinner. He remembered how they'd all been politely appalled when his 'radical' father had served up salad and exotic seafood instead. James McAlpine, whose motto had been *'Tradition is for the gutless and uninspired'*, had been highly amused by the predictable reaction, yet he'd still produced an alternative menu of baked vegetables, roast turkey and pork with all the traditional trimmings.

Growing up, Brett had at times been embarrassed by the fact his parents had rejected most of the middle class values embraced by his peers' families and teachers, who'd viewed his upbringing as being at best unconventional—especially after his mother was arrested at an anti-nuclear rally. Yet now, from the distance of maturity, he could appreciate that James and Kathleen McAlpine had provided their children with a loving and secure environment that went far beyond their material comforts and liberal views on discipline. They'd taught love and tolerance by example, and yet while firmly adhering to their own beliefs had never tried to force feed them to their children.

Yeah, he thought, gazing out at the beach but seeing much more. It had been wonderful growing up here.

As his eyes drifted to the outcrop of rocks at the northern end of the beach yet another time-locked image floated through his mind. One that not only made him smile, but kindled a desire to snatch a piece of the past. But this time, unlike this morning, when he'd dug out his old wetsuit and board, he felt like sharing it.

'Joanna,' he said, 'have you got some ratty old jeans and a pair of runners?'

CHAPTER FOUR

THE mid-morning July air was cool but not cold as they picked their way over moss-covered rocks still damp from the earlier tide.

'Okay, now I know why you wanted me in old clothes and sneakers,' Joanna said. 'But where *exactly* are we going?'

Brett waited until she'd sussed out the width of the rock pool which separated them and then agilely leapt over it before pointing to the wall of rock rising on his right. 'In there.'

'We're going to *climb* the cliff?' Her tone questioned his sanity.

'Nope.' He pulled at a weedy overhanging scrub growing from wide ancient cracks in the upper rockface to reveal a metre-wide cavity at its base. 'We're going to crawl *into* it.'

Shooting him a sceptical look, she crouched to inspect the cave entrance, then frowned over her shoulder at him. 'It's *pitch-black*. We can't go in there.'

'Sure we can…' He fished out the penlight he'd tucked in his back pocket. 'We did all the time as kids.'

'Presumably you were somewhat smaller then,' she said, her gaze running pointedly over him. 'The only way you'd get in there now would be flat on your belly.'

'You got it.'

Watching her mentally assimilate this was a fascinating exercise. A tiny 'V' formed between her perfectly arched eyebrows as she flicked her gaze back to the cave's entrance; a moment later she started to worry her bottom lip with her teeth.

'Is it safe?' she asked, without looking at him.

'Rock-solid,' he said glibly, then added, 'High tide is hours away.'

He dropped onto his knees beside her. 'When we were kids we used to have time trials to see who could get in and out quickest. The record was less than five minutes.'

'Did you hold it?'

'Yep!' He grinned. 'Until my mate Jason broke it. The sub-five time is his. How's the hangover?'

'Shh!' She scowled. 'I'm hoping if I ignore it it'll go away.'

He laughed. 'So how do you want to do this; you want me to lead?'

'Who said I wanted to do it at all?'

'No one.' He grinned again. 'But you have very expressive eyes, Jo, and right now they're practically sparking with anticipation.'

A faint flush hinted at her being pleased by his comment, but she produced a wry smile. 'How do you know it's not fear?'

'Gut instinct,' he responded, privately acknowledging there was a fair bit of sparking going on inside him too. Except in his case he ruefully suspected it owed itself more to Joanna's face being within easy kissing distance rather than the thrill of reliving a boyhood escapade. Damn, but she was beautiful! And yet amazingly she seemed completely unaware of the fact. Too bad he wasn't.

'*Brett*...I asked you a question?'

Yes, she had. He knew because he'd watched her mouth move. Trouble was, what he'd been *imagining* those lush little lips saying had deafened him to what they'd *actually* said. There was probably only one chance in a zillion that a reply of, *You bet I want to make love to you!* wouldn't catch her off guard.

'Sorry, what did you say?' he asked, downshifting his hormones to a lower gear.

'Once we're in there,' she said, pulling a stretchy band

from around her wrist and hastily securing her hair into a ponytail at the top of her head, 'how long will it take us to get to the other side?'

'There is no "other side".'

He watched her mull this over, then again check out what from where they were appeared to be only a narrow tunnel. 'So you're saying we crawl in forwards and then have to come out backwards?'

He shook his head. 'After thirty metres or so the tunnel opens up into a huge cave.'

'So we come out the way we went in?'

He nodded.

'What's in the cave?'

'Nothing.'

Joanna's excited grin created contradictory feelings within him. Most women would have questioned the point in undertaking an exercise which offered no real rewards, and perversely he now half wished Joanna would throw a hissy fit at the whole idea and refuse to take part on the grounds of putting her fingernails at risk. But it seemed Joanna Ford's shy-sexy persona hid a streak of adventure. Discovering she possessed yet another quality the women in his past had lacked was as bothering as it was pleasing. It had him sensing he'd put himself between a rock and hard place even before he'd eased onto his stomach and prepared to snake his way into the damp darkness of the tidal cave.

There was a noticeable but not dramatic drop in temperature within the rock tunnel; the air held the distinct smell of salt and the hard sand-crusted surface beneath his body was still damp from the last high tide. Clasping the flashlight in his right hand, Brett snaked his way forward on his elbows and forearms without once having a problem with the tunnel's vertical clearance. Although width-wise it was an occasional squeeze.

'Don't you dare get stuck,' a muttered voice warned from behind him in one such instance.

'No worries,' he assured her. 'How're you doing?'

'Fine. Just keep going and try not to kick me in the face with those size twelves you're wearing.'

Grinning, he continued to edge forward. 'Almost there. By the way, if you're close enough to read the sizing on the soles of my shoes in this light, you better back off a bit. The floor of the main cave is about a half metre or more below this. I'll have to lower myself down onto my hands to get in there...if you're too close you might get caught by a stray boot.'

'All right.'

When the tunnel finally did open up, the dim, dank surrounds filled Brett with a wave of nostalgia, making him chuckle.

A hand clamped around his right ankle. 'Er, Brett... you're not getting claustrophobic and hysterical on me, are you?'

The cautiously voiced question added to his amusement. 'Nope. Just appreciating some old memories.'

'So how come you've stopped moving?'

'Because I'm at the cave.'

'Already! Really?' The excitement dripping from her voice magnified his own. He wasn't game to examine why.

'Just stay where you are till I get right in, okay?'

'Okay.'

As testament to his increased height since he'd last been down here as a seventeen-year-old, his arms reached the cave floor without being fully extended. He released the flashlight, which rolled a little, throwing patterns of light and shadow on the dark crusty walls, and 'walked' his palms until he could get his feet to the floor. Standing, he turned in a small circle to survey his surroundings.

Structurally nothing had noticeably changed in the almost two decades since his last visit, but it irked him that more recent visitors had found it necessary to make the underground trek armed with spray cans. Unfortunately the absence of skeletal remains suggested the vandals who'd scrawled 'RAP RULES' in fluorescent yellow on the walls hadn't perished from inhaling paint fumes in a confined space.

'Brett! Are you all right?'

'Yeah,' he responded, dusting his gritty hands across the back of his jeans before crouching again at the entrance of the tunnel. 'You can come on through now.'

Joanna's mouth was pursed in concentration as she wormed her way to the end, but by the time she poked her head through at the end it was split into a megawatt grin. 'Hi, there! Just passing; thought I'd drop in…' She looked at the distance to the cave floor. '*Drop* being exactly the word.'

Instinctively Brett took a hold of her forearms. 'It's okay, I've got you. Just ease out slowly.'

'Gotcha,' she said, obeying his instructions, although Brett was pretty sure he hadn't said anything about putting her hands on his shoulders, nor about sliding them around his neck as she emerged further. But, reluctant to look a gift horse in the mouth, and needing to keep his equilibrium, he started inching his feet backwards. Unfortunately Joanna moved forward a fraction too far, at the same time tumbling him first onto his backside, then his back, before landing on top of him with an *'Oomph!'*

Joanna's startled *'Darn!'* was considerably tamer than the four-letter word which burst from him, although he wasn't sure whether her furious blush of embarrassment was caused by his swearing, her part in causing the fall or the suggestive intimacy of how they'd landed. She was stretched between the 'V' of his bent legs, with her belly and breasts pressed tight against him as a result of his arms protectively tightening around her mid-tumble. And it *had* been a purely protective action, he assured himself.

Within seconds, though, she rallied herself. 'Oh, Lord, I'm so sorry!' she gushed. 'It's all my fault. Are you okay?'

Oh, yeah, it was her fault, all right. And he'd be just dandy once she stopped squirming and wriggling her body against his and the stupid voice inside him stopped chanting, *This is your chance; kiss her, kiss her...*

'Brett... Are you going to be able to get up?'

He gave a dry, humourless laugh. 'There's no indication *that's* going to be a problem. Although it's a bit hard with you lying all over me.' *And getting a damn sight harder by the second!* he added silently.

She vaulted off him so fast he half wondered if she'd read his lewd mind, but there was only concern in her face as she watched him scramble to his feet. Once apparently satisfied he showed no signs of being any the worse for their fall, she quickly turned her attention to their surroundings.

'It's brighter in here than I expected it to be,' she observed, trailing her fingers over the wall of the cave as she prowled its perimeter.

'That's because crawling through the tunnel your eyes adjusted to the dimness. Plus, while it's dark looking *into* the cave, from here the exterior sunlight and the tunnel itself works like a skylight.'

She accepted the explanation with a faint nod, then inclined her head towards the graffiti. 'What does this mean?'

'That the future of this planet is in the hands of idiots with no appreciation of nature, no artistic ability and a lousy taste in music.'

She blinked. 'You wrote it as a political statement?'

'Hell, I didn't do it! I stopped scribbling on walls at three and would sooner eat razorblades than listen to rap.'

She looked totally self-conscious as she said, 'Oh, I see...rap is a type of music.'

'Not in my opinion,' he said, astounded that she was apparently ignorant of something intrinsic to most of her age group. 'But then I was raised listening to my folks' Hendrix and Rolling Stones albums.'

'Oh. I've heard some Rolling Stones songs since I've come to Sydney, but I can't remember hearing about a band called Hendrix.'

She *had* to be kidding. He could accept that some people, for unfathomable reasons, didn't appreciate Jimi's awesome talents, but he'd never imagined anyone in western civilisation not knowing the great man's *name*. 'Hendrix isn't a band. He was *the* greatest guitarist to ever live. A genius. I can't believe you haven't heard of him—'

'Well I'm sorry!' she snapped. 'But I can't help that! *I* wasn't raised listening to *any* sort of music.'

For a moment he thought he saw tears in her eyes, but before he could be certain she'd turned away.

'Sorry,' she said. 'I didn't mean to get angry. It's just that I get frustrated by how much I still have to learn. Whenever I think I'm getting to a stage where everything doesn't seem so…so *strange*, I discover there's something else really basic I know absolutely nothing about. I've been living in Sydney for over two months, and I still feel like I've been dumped on another planet.'

'Hey, my fault,' he said, feeling lower than a snake's belly. 'Meaghan told me you'd had a…very protected upbringing.'

'That's one way of putting it, I suppose,' she muttered, before appearing to catch herself and switching on a plastic smile that didn't reach her eyes. 'So, tell me…how'd you and your friends come to discover this cave?'

He would have preferred to explore the reasons for her musically deprived background, but, deciding to ration his insensitivity, accepted the change of subject.

'It wasn't so much a discovery as a kind of inheritance we always knew we'd get,' he told her. 'This has always been a local cubbyhole, and as one generation of kids outgrew it the next adopted it. It's such an accepted progression local parents start drumming the dangers of getting stuck in here with the tide coming in to their kids at the same time they teach them to swim.'

'Has anyone ever been caught?'

'Not that I know of.'

She cast a wistful glance over the bare rock. 'I bet if

these walls could talk, they'd have a few wild tales of mischief to tell. This must've been a great place for parties.'

'Nah,' he said. 'Too hard to get the beer and ice in. Although I wouldn't doubt *some* people might've partaken of the odd cigarette or necking session down here.'

She raised a very expressive eyebrow. 'Anyone I know?'

'I dare say some of the very people you catch the bus with every morning may have misspent their youth here. Of course I wouldn't *dream* of naming names and causing the past to rear its ugly head on people who've grown up to become upstanding citizens.'

'Very noble of you. Guess I'll have to talk to Meaghan. I always learn so much, chatting with her,' she murmured, with a seriousness which might have been believable had she been wearing sunglasses to hide the rank amusement in her eyes.

'Waste of time…she'll never admit to it.'

Wry humour danced across her face. 'Reticence must be a family trait.'

While he couldn't help smiling at her light-hearted teasing, he wasn't comfortable with it. Or rather, he wasn't comfortable with the feelings it aroused within him, because he couldn't make up his mind whether she was being deliberately flirtatious or not. Given the vague details he had on her background, it seemed most likely that she had no idea of the signals she was sending; on the other hand, she *had* had an affair with a married man. Which meant even though she'd been unaware he was married she'd presumably had to have been better than useless in the sack to keep his interest and—*whoa!*

Brett brought his wayward thoughts to a halt so fast he could practically smell rubber. Joanna Ford was just a naive country kid who'd already been taken for a ride by one jerk, she sure didn't need to encounter another one.

Silently cursing whatever nostalgia-induced insanity had motivated him to suggest this excursion in the first place, he curtly announced it was time to head back… And it didn't bother him one bit that those clear turquoise eyes dulled with disappointment.

'Are toasted sandwiches okay with you? Or would you prefer something more filling?'

Joanna's question caught him off guard. However, her shower-fresh, head-to-foot fashion-plate appearance resolved his curiosity about what she'd been doing for the last eighty minutes since they'd returned to the house.

'More filling?' he echoed, trying to convince his brain that now he *did* want it to focus on Joanna after spending the last hour telling it the opposite.

'Mmm,' she said, giving a brief glance to the headline of the Saturday paper, which he'd discarded on the coffee table in favour of the real estate supplement. 'I could cook something if you want.'

'Why?' he asked absently, speculating whether the smooth line of her tight leggings over her backside was the result of a G-string or absolutely nothing at all. He virtuously banished the thought the instant he realised she was staring at him with the look of someone fearful they were dealing with a complete idiot.

'Er...run that by me again,' he said, forcing an apologetic but hopefully intelligent smile.

She shook her head, her smile patient. 'One minute you've got your head in a cave and the next you've got it stuck in the clouds.'

After a brief, hard-fought victory over the first response which rose to his lips—*'Clouds be damned, my head was in your pants!'*—he merely shrugged. 'Well, you know jet lag can kind of linger on.'

'No, I don't. I've never been on a plane in my life.' A broad grin transformed her face. 'But believe me, it's right up near the top of my list of things I have to do!'

If the enthusiasm in her smile had been radioactive Brett figured the entire room would be glowing. 'I see...and what has top position on your "things you have to do" list?'

'Right now it's to make your lunch.' She wrinkled her nose. 'So help me out here, and hurry up and decide what you want before I have to leave.'

Her hands-on-hips assertiveness didn't grab his attention as much as it previously might have. 'You're going somewhere?'

'A football game between the Manly Sea Eagles and the Parramatta Seals.'

'The Parramatta *Eels*,' he corrected automatically.

'Oh. Right... *Eels*, not seals.' She momentarily closed her eyes, as if committing a life-essential piece of information to memory. 'I've never been to a rugby league game before, so I don't really care who wins,' she went on to confide. 'But I've been told Manly is the local team, so I guess I better cheer for them. Is that your team?'

'I used to follow them.'

'Why'd you change?'

'I didn't. It's just I've been overseas four years. I take it you're going with the guy from last night?' Brett hadn't meant to voice the comment, certainly not in the surly-sounding way it had come out.

She frowned. 'What guy?'

'The jerk who brought you home so plastered you could barely stand up and then left you out the front.'

Her eyes widened at his terse response, but instead of getting angry she seemed even more confused. 'That's what they always do when they bring me home. And why on earth would I be going to the football game with a cab driver?'

He bounded to his feet. 'Cab driver? You came home in a *taxi* last night?'

'How else was I going to get home?' she asked, tilting her head to peer up at him every bit as intently as he was peering down at her. 'I was too sick to catch a bus, even if they hadn't already stopped running.'

'You were *drunk*, not sick.'

'Not on purpose!' she objected.

'I know that,' he muttered, uncertain why he felt so angry or whom the anger was directed at. 'Why the devil didn't you insist the guy who picked you up take you home?'

'Hey!' She poked a finger into his chest. Judging by the high-voltage electrical charge that went through him, her other hand was shoved in a power outlet. 'I didn't get *picked up* by anyone!'

'That's a lie!'

'*Excuse me?*'

'Listen, I *saw* you getting into some bloke's Porsche and—'

'Oh!'

'Yes, *oh!* Now—'

'That was Bianca's car,' she cut in, her voice tinged with amusement.

'Bianca?'

'One of the models from work. It was one of her friends' parties and when I said I didn't think I'd go because I had no way of getting there she offered to drive me. I misunderstood you,' she added. 'I thought you meant picked up as in…well, you know…'

'As in a guy hitting on you,' he supplied sheepishly. *How stupid did he feel now?* 'I had my wires crossed too,' he admitted, in the hope of redeeming himself. 'I have a real thing about guys who can't be bothered showing a woman to her door. Although it's a bit much to expect from a cab driver…'

A shy smile parted her lips. It amazed him how she could switch from looking blazing mad one second to utterly serene the next. More amazing still was how she could set his blood on fire regardless of whether she was being tempestuous or tranquil. How was it he barely knew this woman and yet she activated both his passion and his protective instincts as no other had? And *ludicrous* was the only word to describe the level of relief he felt at finding out her "date" last night hadn't been male. Of course that raised another question…who was she going to the football with today?

There were plenty of models who'd try for the opportunity of getting close to a high-profile footballer in the hope of snatching a little of the spotlight, but usually they scouted the talent in the league club *after* games. Of course, there were women who genuinely enjoyed watching the game for its own sake…or so he'd heard; he'd never been lucky enough to meet one himself.

'So, what time's Bianca picking you up?' he asked, with what he considered praiseworthy casualness considering they were still standing only inches apart and her hand still rested on his chest. However, gazing down to where her touch was initiating the anarchy between his conscience and his hormones alerted her to the situation.

'Huh? Oh! No!' she said, hastily withdrawing her hand as she stepped away. 'That is, I don't think Bianca is coming. She vanished from the party before the idea was suggested. I'm going with another girl and her boyfriend and his cousin.'

A single male cousin, he'd bet!

'Look, Brett…' She shifted from one foot to the other, her tone splintered with agitation. 'I'm going to have to start getting ready soon, so it'd help if you could decide what you want for lunch.'

'Nothing,' he said, telling himself it wasn't that he'd lost his appetite but a case of not being hungry for food in the first place. 'You just go get ready.'

'Don't be silly. You have to eat. And it's my turn to cook. So tell me, what do you feel like having?'

He was poised to respond with, *I feel like having you,* when she glanced out of the window and emitted a half-shriek, half-gasp.

'Oh, no! They're early! They aren't supposed to be here until a quarter past one.'

Brett pointed to the clock on the living room wall which announced it was five minutes after that, and she grimaced.

Although that could have been due to the blast of the air-horn from the almost entirely chromed classic Monaro currently idling, loudly but perfectly, in the driveway.

'Want me to entertain them while you get ready?'

'Oh, thank you!' she exclaimed, flinging her arms around his waist.

Before he had a chance to recognise and react to the opportunity kicking his proverbial door open, an obviously equally stunned Joanna was backing away at light speed and stammering almost as fast.

'I...ah...um. Tell them I...won't be long. And...and I'm sorry. A-about lunch and...' Her blush turned several shades redder. 'And...and, well, I...promise I'll...cook next time.'

Some ten minutes later she was all cool, calm chic in Jackie Kennedy-style sunglasses and a camel-coloured hip-length coat, which presumably covered *something*, if not her Lycra-clad legs and those damn thigh-high boots. Which, not surprisingly, had her two sub-twenty-five-year-old male escorts practically drooling and the equally young blonde female trying desperately not to scowl. Meaning Brett and the blonde had something in common.

Having chatted with the threesome while they'd waited for Joanna, Brett decided that, given his own past, there was no reason to suspect the guys' youthful enthusiasm for cars, parties, booze, football and, presumably, sex meant they weren't perfectly normal, decent guys who in a few years would be firmly entrenched in sedate middle class marriages. Although that assumption didn't ease the temptation to tell them he didn't want them within ten miles of Joanna.

Knowing his possessiveness was unjustified, not to mention irrational, he drew on all the maturity, intelligence and common sense he'd acquired in the last dozen years of his life and moved fast enough to help Joanna into the car before either of the other two men could. Then once again he complimented the driver on the immaculate condition of his car, politely shook both men's hands, saying it was good meeting them, wished one and all an enjoyable afternoon and waited until they'd reversed out of the drive before walking back inside. Where he proceeded to fix himself a toasted cheese sandwich while simultaneously hoping for the pristine car to blow a head gasket.

CHAPTER FIVE

BRETT decided it was a good thing he wasn't a cat or a dog, because if he'd had to depend on Joanna feeding him he'd have starved to death!

He didn't sight her again over the weekend after she went to the football, although the scent of her perfume in the bathroom on Sunday morning suggested she *had* come home at some stage. On Monday she'd left for work before he was up, and some time during the day, while he'd been out scouting local real estate agents, she'd left a message on the answering machine saying she'd be late home. The same thing had happened on Tuesday.

Not that her absence bothered him, Brett assured himself. But either Meaghan was shelling out a bundle in overtime or his phantom housemate had one hell of a social life. Then again, why wouldn't she? She was young, single and painfully attractive; it'd be at least four or five years before she tired of the frenetic pace of trying to combine the party and nightclub scenes with a career.

Whereas here he was today, heading home after having spent the morning with the staff of his mother's company, lunch with the owner and general manager of a national television network and the afternoon inspecting four different houses with four different realtors in four different suburbs. About the only recreational activity he was looking forward to was sinking his teeth into the pizza on the passenger seat then catching the late-night news before bed. Of course he wouldn't have minded a little company too, but he hadn't been able to motivate himself enough to return the interest of the redhead who'd been working her cute little butt off at the pub trying to chat him up. And the reason for that was Toni, *no one else*.

His first thought at the sight of his sister's car parked haphazardly at the front of the house was that he'd have some company after all and that he should've ordered a bigger pizza. The second had him pressing down on the accelerator…

He entered the house to the sound of a *three*-way female discussion about whether Meaghan should or shouldn't have bought the coat she'd tried on in Armani's. They hadn't reached a consensus by the time he walked into the kitchen and interrupted them.

His sister and niece greeted him with a casual enthusiasm that included demanding to know what kind of pizza they'd be having. The raven-haired witch standing next to the stove-top, ignoring the squealing whistle of the kettle, merely produced an uncertain smile and asked if he wanted tea or coffee.

If hearing her voice on his arrival had lightened his spirits, seeing her had them all but floating. Which perversely bothered him, because he'd pretty much convinced himself this girl held no interest for him. None.

Besides, he reasoned silently, if he *had* been interested in Joanna, or her unexplained activities of the three previous nights, he could easily have extracted the information from his sister under cover of enquiring how things were at the agency. The fact he hadn't done so seemed to prove his curiosity about his rarely sighted housemate was waning. Good. She was way too young for him, and even if she wasn't, he wasn't interested in complicating his life right now with another relationship. He wasn't.

'Brett! Are you listening to me?'

Meaghan's impatient tone and expression dragged his eyes away from the brunette engaged in the fascinating act of standing on tiptoe to lift mugs from the top shelf of the cupboard. *Lycra bodysuits and short skirts were definitely the fashion world's greatest contribution—to men.*

'Huh? Oh, sorry. I was thinking about a block of land I looked at today.' Well, he *had* looked at several potential building sites. At Meaghan's sceptically raised eyebrow he tacked on, 'It was up at North Palm. Heaps of potential. I'm going to get Jason's opinion on it when he gets back from Melbourne.'

'Well, right now it's *your* opinion I want, brother dear. That—'

'You've got it, and it's good,' he responded glibly, dropping the pizza box on the table and his backside onto the nearest chair.

'Cute. But I hadn't finished. I also need your time—*and presence*—at the agency.'

'No way!' he said vehemently. 'Absolutely not. I told you, I'm not interested in taking an active interest.'

'I'm not asking for a lifetime commitment,' she said, nodding as Karessa announced she was going in to catch the end of a medical series on TV. 'I just want you to sit in on a couple of meetings I've got planned.'

'No go.' He shook his head for added emphasis and caught Joanna watching him with a kind of wistful curiosity. When she realised he'd noted her interest she quickly busied herself with pouring the coffee.

'Brett, *please*.' Meaghan switched from bossy to pleading with practised smoothness. He wondered if this trait was inherent to all sisters or if his was merely particularly gifted. 'This is *really* important to me. To *us*.'

'Why?' he asked, more interested in the shy, uncertain smile Joanna bestowed on him as she placed his coffee on the table. While her fair skin and raven hair gave her an exotic, dramatic look in the basic black she always seemed to wear, Brett wondered if she had any idea how magnificent she'd look draped in a sheet the same colour as her eyes. He'd had sheets that colour once...

'Brett!'

He started guiltily and hoped his sister's glare meant she hadn't added mind-reading to her vices. 'What?'

'Look, I know you aren't fussed with getting involved with the agency, but this is too crucial a matter for you to ignore,' Meaghan told him.

'I think it'd be best,' Joanna said softly, 'if I left you two to discuss this in private.'

'There's no need for that, Joanna,' Meaghan countered. 'Sit down. You're already aware of what's going on. The thing is, Brett…'

Brett looked from his sister to the hovering Joanna, who hesitated for long seconds then took the seat beside him so reluctantly that he had to wonder whether Meaghan was about to announce the possibility of financial ruin or if his deodorant was letting him down. Joanna, on the other hand, carried the same alluring scent which invariably had his hormones twitching. He took a mouthful of scalding coffee to distract them. It was painful but effective therapy, and dragged his attention back to his sister, seated opposite.

'I've taken Meaghan's as far as I can in Sydney,' she was saying. 'Financially we're in a position to capitalise on that success. Doing this is the next logical step. You *must* see that, Brett.'

He had no idea what it was he should be seeing, but the expectant stare he was getting hinted that Meaghan considered she'd made things perfectly clear. Damn! He didn't know what perfume Joanna wore, but it could double as a mind-washing chemical. In a bid to counter it, he lifted the lid on the pizza.

'Well, Meaghan,' he said, fishing for a response that wouldn't show his lack of attention, 'the agency's success is entirely due to your management, so I'm more than happy to trust your judgement on this. You've managed for four years without my input; I don't see why you feel you need my opinion.'

'Fine, then!' His sister cut him off with haughty curtness. 'I was only acting out of professional courtesy, but if you're happy to let me invest close to a million bucks of the company's money cold—'

'What?' His amazement clashed with a breathy gasp from the woman on his left, who'd had him so distracted he'd clearly missed vital chunks of whatever his sister had said. But he also knew the mention of a sum *that* large wouldn't have escaped his notice even if Joanna had stripped naked. Well, okay, maybe under those ideal circumstances he *might* have missed it, but unfortunately the lady beside him was still very much clothed. His sister, however, was on her feet and pacing the room with theatrical earnestness.

'Expansion makes sense, Brett. And even if we weren't in such good shape I couldn't *not* consider this deal. This is opportunity virtually *storming* the door. To ignore it would be lunacy, especially now the agency is perfectly poised to move to a higher level. After all, how often does the chance to buy into a London-based modelling agency present itself?'

'Mercifully, not often,' he muttered dryly. Then decided to try reason. 'Meaghan, at the risk of sounding conservative, don't you think it would be better to expand on a more local scale first, like Melbourne or New Zealand?'

'No!' she said. 'Oh, I know we've only just cleared all our establishment debts and all, but…this is a *golden* opportunity, Brett. We'd have international connections that'd mean local models would be falling over themselves to sign with us.'

That was all well and good, but Brett was more interested in ensuring that if things didn't work out they wouldn't get tripped up on bankruptcy. 'What about the financial ramifications for us?'

'I've already spoken to our accountant,' she told him. 'The thing is, if things go as I expect, you'll be looking for more tax breaks inside two years.'

He could recognise Meaghan being evasive or 'creatively truthful' a mile off. 'Okay, now tell me *exactly* what the accountant said on the subject,' he said.

His comment drew an amused chuckle from Joanna and

a dismissive wave from his sister. 'Brett, he's an *account-ant* for God's sake. He thinks it's a risk to keep more than ten dollars in petty cash. All that really matters is he agrees that financially we can *afford* to do this. You can ask him yourself,' she told him. 'Of course, what he doesn't understand is why we can't afford *not* to do it.'

'In other words, he's not foaming at the mouth with excitement at the idea.'

'Brett, the potential this has for us is enormous. Bigger than enormous. You *must* see that?'

There was no denying her excitement or passion for the project, but it wouldn't be the first time Meaghan had been excited or passionate about something that wasn't in her best interests. His sister was notorious for following her impulses rather than her common sense—something he knew she privately feared, even if she wouldn't publicly admit it. So, for all that Meaghan was pushing to sell him on this deal, Brett knew that if she'd been a hundred per cent confident she was doing the right thing she wouldn't have invited him to play devil's advocate. Meaghan's projected image of being totally self-confident was more often than not only skin-deep. A defence mechanism developed in the wake of the emotional demolition job the bastard who'd got her pregnant had done on her.

The surge of brotherly love and pride that rose in him as he remembered how hard Meaghan had struggled to put her life back together took some of the edge off the anger he still carried over what had been done to her. It also stopped him from sticking to his plan of having nothing to do with the agency.

He sighed, reluctantly accepting his fate. 'When and where are these meetings you want me to attend?'

His sister's face broke into a broad grin. 'One's tomorrow at nine o'clock. At the agency. We should be finished by midday at the latest. But if that's going to be a problem for you I could try and reschedule it.'

He held up a hand to halt the enthusiastic babble. 'Relax,

Meaghan. As it happens, tomorrow's fine.' It wasn't, but he could rearrange the appointment he had with an architect friend of his father's.

'Great!' she exclaimed. 'And, Joanna, since Brett will be driving in, don't worry about starting at eight-thirty. You can come in whenever he does and save yourself a bus trip...'

The front seat of his mother's Honda coupé had never felt so claustrophobic, and he could literally feel the tension radiating from the passenger side seat. Though they'd shared a pot of coffee at breakfast, the conversation hadn't exceeded mutual good mornings, and the scintillating exchange of, 'What time will you be ready to leave?'

'Whenever you say.'

'Seven o'clock, okay?'

'Fine. Thanks.'

Now, at two minutes past the designated departure time, they were negotiating the winding Palm Beach Road in a thick, stilted silence. The last time Brett recalled being tongue-tied around a female he'd been thirteen and awe-struck by the smile of fifteen-year-old Kylie Peters. Back then his awkwardness had stemmed from the fact that he didn't know how to deliver a smooth pick-up line; now it existed because he realised he didn't know how *not* to. While it was no use denying he found the shy, reticent Joanna extremely attractive, his conscience was having a hard time letting go of the fact she was twelve years his junior and even younger in experience. Hell, when he'd been having wet dreams about delectable Kylie, the now even more delectable Ms Joanna Ford had been wearing diapers!

Further complicating things was the guilty recognition that he'd agreed to attend this meeting today more out of a desire to spend time with Joanna than a desire to oblige his sister. Then again, his sister was the one who'd placed this hot little brunette off-limits to him, so it wasn't as if he was predisposed to being all that obliging to her anyway!

'Thanks for the lift. It sure beats the bus.'

The husky sound of Joanna's voice caused his pulse to trip and him to veer slightly onto the wrong side of the road. Peripherally he saw her clutch the dashboard.

'You and Meaghan had the same driving instructor, huh?' Her calm, ironically delivered aside made him burst out laughing.

Risking his pulse-rate further, he looked across at her. 'Yeah. But the difference is I *listened* to him.' Looking back to the road, he added, 'I hope you aren't trying to copy Meaghan's driving style too closely.'

She smiled. 'Actually, I'm thinking of enrolling with a driving school. I'm just not sure how to tell her without hurting her feelings. She and your mother have been very good to me.'

'Why not tell her that since we're living in the same house and she's got to come out of her way you've decided it'll be simpler if I took over giving you lessons?' He was as taken aback by his suggestion as Joanna seemed to be. Wonderful! His libido was assuming the role of his brain.

'No…I couldn't do that; I couldn't lie to her.'

'It's only a lie if you're not doing it.'

'You…you mean you'd really do that? Give up your time to give me lessons?'

Brett gritted his teeth to keep from telling her what else he'd be prepared to give up to be able to tutor her in other directions. 'Sure. No problem.'

It was a moment before she said, 'Well, okay, then. Thanks.'

The smile she gave him was dazzling, and had him gripping the steering wheel far tighter than *any* driving instructor would recommend. Talk about buying himself more trouble!

'Meaghan's really pleased you're getting involved with

the business,' she said, with the air of one who wasn't sure if she was speaking out of turn or not.

'Mmm. Well, I'm glad *she's* happy,' he grumbled. 'Frankly, the less time I have to spend at the damn agency the better.'

'Would it help if I offered to run interference if any of our clients get out of hand?'

The hesitant, cryptic offer had him shooting her a questioning look. Just when she'd opened her mouth to explain, the penny dropped in what Brett had once regarded as his better than average brain.

'No! Let me guess…' he said sourly. 'My sister has recounted the details of my recent disastrous love life and my aversion to models.'

'Karessa, actually,' she corrected.

'Karessa. Wonderful. Glad to know I can rely on all members of my family to air my private life.'

'Oh, she wasn't gossiping,' she said quickly. 'Actually, she was just trying to reassure me. I was thinking of finding somewhere else to stay.'

He swung to face her. '*You're moving out?* But you can't! What about the driving lessons?' It was probably the most inane comment he'd ever made, but she didn't seem to notice.

'Oh, no! Not *now*. It's just that, not really knowing you, I wasn't very comfortable about sharing a house with you. And, well…to be honest, that's why I've been avoiding you.'

'*Avoiding* me?' The words came out with a hint of the desperation he was feeling.

'I've been deliberately staying out late so I didn't have to be alone with you,' she confessed. 'I'm sorry. But now that everything's out in the open and I know I can trust you, well… I'll be home more often.'

Oh, swell! She trusted him! Just the sort of pressure a guy needed in this situation!

'I meant what I said about taking turns with meals,' she

continued. 'And if it's okay with you I thought I'd cook dinner tonight.'

Dinner? Brett doubted he'd ever have an appetite again. Talk about being put in a moral vice. Here he was with his hormones running amok and she *trusted* him. Well, bloody great! That made one of them!

Brett figured they were waiting for the slowest moving elevator in the world as he again tried to put some distance between himself and a leggy blonde who, if she got any closer, would give him a chill from the breeze of her batting eyelashes. Had he thought the consternation on Joanna's face stemmed from jealousy, he'd have played up to the slinky model for all he was worth, but he *knew* her disapproval wasn't that personal. Joanna felt safe with him. She *trusted* him.

'Carla,' she said, addressing the model, who was now fingering Brett's lapels and trying to convince him they should get together for drinks, 'aren't you due at a shoot in the city?'

'That's not till two.'

'Oh. Sorry, I didn't realise they'd rescheduled it again.' Carla flicked an irritated frown at her. 'What do you mean, *again*? It's always been two.'

'Oh?' Joanna sounded bemused. 'I was sure Meaghan mentioned something about the Mundle shoot being changed.' The turquoise eyes that met Brett's were full of mischief. 'Guess it was another one.'

'Mundle...Mundle,' he said, picking up on Joanna's cue. 'No, I'm pretty certain that's the one she said was changed.'

'Well, damn it!' The blonde's interest in him vanished. 'Why wasn't *I* told?' she demanded of a brilliantly puzzled-looking Joanna.

'I don't know, Carla, I'm only the receptionist. Maybe you should check with Jeff Corbet?'

'Check with him!' the model fumed, taking long strides towards the far end of the corridor. 'I'm going to kill him!'

When the elevator doors swooshed open Joanna leaned past him to peer inside. 'All clear,' she said, stepping back to lob him a teasing smile. 'Think you're safe riding up to the third floor alone?'

Glad to again be the recipient of the teasing banter he'd been missing since their excursion to the cave, he grinned. 'Can't hurt to live dangerously once in a while, I guess.'

Today her hair was swept up into a retro style that left a thick gelled strand hanging loose and half covering her left eye as she gazed up at him. Brett fisted his hands to defeat the urge to reach out and hook it behind her ear. While he was genetically predisposed to being fashion conscious himself, preferring casual designer clothes to jeans and sweats, it seemed sinful that a face as uniquely beautiful as Joanna's should be even semi-shrouded.

The elevator doors started to close, prodding them from their silent regard of each other; Brett reflexively threw out a hand to stall them.

'Well, I'd best get to the front desk,' Joanna said, hiking her leather backpack higher onto her shoulder. 'Thanks for the ride and—'

'What time do you have lunch?' The question was out before Brett realised he'd even had the thought. Still, he told himself, having lunch with her was an utterly benign exercise.

There was a slight pause before she answered. 'One-thirty, unless there's a drama. But of course,' she added, 'around here that's more the norm than not.'

'Well, how about we both try and steer clear of dramas until then? If we manage it, lunch will be my treat.' Sensing she was going to utter a protest, he produced his most winning smile of appeal. 'Hey, I owe you for rescuing me from the clutches of the designing Carla...'

Brett made the short ride upstairs slumped against the wall of the small compartment, mentally picturing her smiling nod of acceptance and ignoring the nagging voice telling him that inviting her to lunch was courting trouble—

when he wasn't supposed to be interested in *courting* anything. But, hey, it was no big deal. Not really. He'd had lunch with plenty of women he'd had no desire to hit on—his sister, his mother, his niece and…and, well, *countless* others whose names he couldn't recall simply because sharing lunch with them had been of no real consequence. *Just as having lunch with Joanna was no big deal!*

It wasn't. He had no intention of getting embroiled in another personal relationship and certainly not with a kid Joanna's age. So he was worrying about nothing. No, he *wasn't* worrying! Having lunch with Joanna wasn't going to be any more stressful than having lunch with Karessa. He was merely being unusually paranoid as a result of the Toni fiasco and perceiving problems with women where there was absolutely no chance of them existing.

He stepped out of the elevator on the third floor, telling himself the only problem he faced was the imminent business meeting… *Damn*, he was a lousy liar.

CHAPTER SIX

'WHEN you offered to buy me lunch I thought you meant a hamburger. I'm never going to be able to eat all this in an hour.'

Brett was still so enamoured by the dazzling smile Joanna had been wearing since they'd walked in the door of the elegant Chinese restaurant that it took him a moment to realise their meal had been placed on the table. Though aromatic and beautifully presented, it didn't look anywhere near as delicious as the woman opposite him.

'You've only got to eat half of it; I'll take care of the rest.'

'It'll still be a challenge. I don't know how to use chopsticks.'

'Well, there's no time like the present to learn. Here, I'll show you.'

After demonstrating the technique several times, by taking food from the assorted dishes and filling each of their plates, Brett encouraged her to try. Predictably, her first few attempts were clumsy, but eventually she was managing to get every third or fourth load to her mouth.

'You're making me do this so that you get more, aren't you?' she accused when a piece of satay beef failed to make it to her mouth after several attempts. 'You're using those things with ten times the speed and success I am.'

'Understandable, since I've been using them since before I could talk.'

'Really?'

'Nah, not that early, but before I started school at any rate,' he amended, discreetly signalling the waiter. 'Dad was fanatical about any and all Asian food, but especially Chinese. We even had a Chinese cook once.'

Her smile faltered and she slowly shook her head. 'You have no idea of the difficulty I have imagining what it must've been like for you and Meaghan growing up. My own upbringing was so…different.'

The cautious statement presented an opportunity to discover more about her first-hand, but the appearance of the waiter halted the immediate pursuit of his curiosity. 'The lady would like a knife and fork, please.'

'Brett,' she whispered, flushing furiously.

'What?'

His genuine confusion put him on the receiving end of an irritated glare before she turned an apologetic expression to the waiter. 'I'm so sorry to seem rude. But it's just that I haven't used chopsticks before.'

'There's no need to apologise, madam,' the waiter said. 'It's a common request.'

'Oh.' The barely whispered word would've been a clue to her embarrassment even if her colour hadn't risen again.

'I swear you're the only woman I know who blushes.'

'Probably because I'm the only woman you know who's so completely ignorant of basic day-to-day knowledge.'

'Hey, I was paying you a *compliment*.'

'Oh…well, er, thank you.' She seemed so surprised that he had to wonder if it was because she'd never been complimented before or had merely expected less of him.

'Still,' she said, 'if you know a way of *preventing* one's self from blushing I'd like to know it.'

He shook his head. 'Can't help you. I suspect the only way is to become really hard-edged and jaded…and I wouldn't like to see that happen to you.'

The waiter had returned with the requested knife and fork on a small tray. After setting it down, he proceeded to present Joanna with a sealed set of chopsticks. At her questioning look, he smiled. 'I thought madam might like to practise at home.'

'Oh, I would! Thank you. Thank you very much.'

Her delight was such Brett could only nod in agreement

when the waiter murmured, 'My pleasure, madam. "Hard-edged and jaded" is nothing new to me; your sincerity and thoughtfulness is.'

It was for Brett, too, yet he couldn't manage to contain his laughter as Joanna's embarrassment manifested itself in the usual manner.

'Stop it,' she said, her own voice corrupted by humour. 'I'm convinced one day every blood vessel in my face will explode.'

Once she had utensils she was familiar with, Joanna was more at ease, and enthusiastically tried all of the seven dishes on the table. It made a pleasant change to dine with a woman who didn't want to estimate the number of calories in every morsel of food on her fork and wasn't coy about stating what she liked and disliked about each one—her opinion of his favourite Mongolian lamb being that it was okay, but only if you were desperate to have your sinuses cleared.

'You're exaggerating,' he told her. 'It's not *that* hot.'

'Maybe not, if you're used to it, but unlike you I don't have a Chinese cook in my past.'

He seized the moment. 'So, what *do* you have in your past?'

The radiance of her mood dimmed. 'Nothing very exciting.'

Those three sadly flat words hung alone for so long Brett wanted to kick himself for ruining what up till now had been one of the most enjoyable meals he'd ever shared. They'd chattered and laughed over a host of inconsequential things, and if that was what it took to keep her smiling, then he'd stick to light-hearted topics. He was frantically searching his mind to come up with something when she spoke again.

'My parents were always very strict and very narrow-minded,' she said, her eyes watching her right hand play with her water glass.

'Or at least they were with me,' she qualified. 'I don't

know what they were like when my older sister Faith was growing up, but she was twenty-three when I was born, and like an extra parent to me anyway.' She sighed. 'I was one of those change-of-life babies; Mother was forty-five when she had me and Father was ten years older than her.'

It struck Brett that she didn't use the formal terms 'Mother' and 'Father' with the type of snobbish intonation of respect the aristocracy bred into their kids, but in an empty, remote sort of tone. If he'd been pressed to try and attach any emotional inflection to them, then he might have said there was a hint of regret present.

Sensing he'd learn more with subtle encouragement than probing, he swallowed his multitude of questions with a mouthful of green tea.

'Father was a very religious man,' she said. 'He adhered to the Bible in the strictest possible way, insisting we read it morning and evening before we ate. On Sundays and Holy days it was also read at lunch, plus an extra hour of prayer in the morning and evening.'

She sighed. 'Don't worry about trying not to look amazed,' she said, picking up on the incredulity he hadn't been able to hide. 'I know it's not normal.'

Unsure whether she meant 'normal' as in *usual* or 'normal' as in *sane behaviour*, he refrained from saying, *You're telling me!*

'Father wasn't very tolerant of anything modern. We weren't allowed to play music, or have a television or magazines. I was eleven before I even saw a TV programme.'

This time Brett couldn't contain himself. '*Eleven.* But what about your schoolfriends? Surely they had TVs; you must've seen them when you slept over at their house or went to birthday parties and such?'

The simple directness of her gaze more or less told him the answer to that even before she did. 'I didn't go to parties or sleep-overs, Brett.

'To make friends at school or anywhere else you have

to have popularity and the opportunity to cultivate those friendships. I had neither. I wasn't permitted to mix with other students outside of school, which meant I didn't have anything in common with them *at* school. It didn't help that I was a naturally good student, or that because the teachers felt sorry for me they tended to give me extra attention.'

'Geez, just what every kid craves—the extra attention of teachers.'

He'd hoped for more than the sadly ironic smile his facetiousness drew. He wanted those turquoise eyes re-ignited with the excitement they'd held when she'd first entered the restaurant, the sheer delight they'd portrayed over something as simple as a gift of cellophane-wrapped chopsticks.

'Actually, I was grateful to the teachers,' she said. 'Which I guess indicates how different I was to normal kids. But they used to leave the library unlocked at lunchtimes so I could sneak in and read all the books I wasn't allowed to read at home but which were essential to the syllabus. At other times I used to pore over the atlases and encyclopedias, learning about countries and customs I'd never imagined existed.'

'*Books you weren't allowed to read...*' Brett frowned. 'I don't understand. I take it we're not talking *Penthouse* and *Playboy*, here?'

The comment made her laugh. 'You know, until I started working at the agency I didn't even know what those magazines were. If anyone had asked me I'd have assumed they were about toys for rich men and architecture.'

'Well, you'd have been right on one count.'

She raised an eyebrow. 'I'm not sure many of the girls at the agency would appreciate that comment.'

'Probably not. But then I'm not interested in winning the approval of any of the girls at the agency...' He deliberately let the sentence dangle, but regretted the action when she shifted uncomfortably. He tried to salvage the conversation. 'So what *were* the books you couldn't read?'

'Anything my father deemed ungodly or immoral. Which included just about everything from Shakespeare to comic books. No magazines of any description were allowed in the house and he vetted the daily papers. Those articles he felt we should read were cut out for us; the rest he burned.'

The entire concept of such a dictatorial parent was beyond Brett. 'But what about your mother? Surely she didn't *approve* of all this?'

'Genesis 3:16 sums up my mother's whole life.'

His expression gave him away, because before he could ask, she said, 'It states to the wife "…in sorrow thou shalt bring forth children; and thy desire shall be to thy husband, and he shall rule over thee."' She sighed. 'That was the beginning and the end of my mother's existence.'

There wasn't a lot he could say. At least nothing that was tactful.

'Moving to Sydney has been like moving to another planet,' she told him.

'You like it?'

It was hard to tell what was brighter, her broad, unabashed grin or the flare of glee shining in her eyes. 'I *love* it,' she said, her voice hushed with passion. 'It's so big and so bright. Loud and exciting. So wild, yet sophisticated. For the first time I feel like I'm really alive, you know; like I'm *part* of something.'

She laughed, shaking her head. 'I know that must sound really childish to you…' There was no apology in her tone. 'But to someone who craved to travel the world and had never been permitted to go anywhere but school without her parents, this is like…well, I don't know…' Again she laughed. 'Like having your first taste of Belgian chocolate and knowing you've still got a whole box of the stuff to get through!'

He laughed. 'Let me guess… My mum introduced you to the chocolate?'

'Mmm. And that's only one of the things for which she'll have my eternal gratitude. I like your mother,' she added.

'So do I, when she's not trying to force her business onto me,' he said dryly.

'Ingrate,' she said pleasantly. 'It could have been a feed and grain store.'

'Meaghan said you'd inherited the family business. Is your sister running it alone now?' *Wrong question!* his brain chided as she momentarily stiffened.

'I guess so. I don't know. We haven't kept in contact. Or at least Faith hasn't.' Her voice tightened. 'I've sent her a dozen letters since I started working for Meaghan and she hasn't answered one. Even though we didn't part on good terms I was hoping we might be able to stay in touch. I suspect it's time to chalk that idea up as a failure.' Though she worked hard at appearing unaffected it didn't come off.

'Some people aren't much for letter-writing,' he said, not to excuse the sister but in the hope of lightening her again shadowed eyes.

'It's not that,' she said softly, her gaze now downcast. 'Faith still adheres to my parents' beliefs. She's not ignoring me because she's too busy to write, but because I had an affair with a married man.' Her head came up and she looked him squarely in the eye. 'By the standards I was raised with…I'm morally corrupt.'

He was struck momentarily speechless by two things. The first was that she'd made the statement without even a trace of self-consciousness. The second thing was that she'd even made the statement!

'What a load of crap!' he exploded, startling not only Joanna but the diners at nearby tables. He lowered his voice. 'You can't really believe that, Joanna? You *can't*,' he insisted.

'No…' she said. 'I don't. Not any more. But it's what Faith believes. And because she does I'm estranged from the only member of my family still living.'

Brett was about to point out that, all things considered,

she ought to be counting her blessings, but Joanna was on her feet before he got the chance.

'I better get going or I'll be late. Thank you for lunch. I really enjoyed it.'

Her breath-defying smile flashed at him, warm and sincere, and it was a few seconds before he sufficiently recovered from its impact to have her wait while he paid the bill.

They parted company at her reception desk, only because some model arrived sobbing over the fact that she'd just missed out on a job and was determined to air her ideas of possible suicide methods to a too sympathetic Joanna. Brett wondered whether if he voiced the idea of buying razorblades in the same breath as bemoaning that he too would never grace the catwalks of Paris Jo would send some of those whispered reassurances and consoling hugs his way.

Of course, the most ironic thing about the whole situation was watching Joanna take the maternal role with a woman who he guessed was probably five years older and light years more experienced than she was. Then again, he'd learned at lunch that experience and maturity were relevant things. For all Joanna's worldly innocence, her childhood had been bizarrely unchildlike. And thanks to some jerk who'd taken advantage of the results of that childhood, and a sister who'd branded her morally corrupt, her entry into adulthood hadn't been any picnic either.

By rights he'd have expected her to be resentful of her sister and withdrawn and distrustful of people. Instead, she was deeply hurt because she couldn't re-establish contact with someone who'd shut her out of their life in the cruellest possible way. Yet, as angry as he was at the way Jo had been treated, he couldn't help feeling pleased and flattered that she'd revealed intimate details of her life to him with a frankness and trust that instinctively made him want to prove them well placed.

He groaned at the irrefutable evidence that Murphy's Law and irony were the ruling cosmic influences in his life.

He'd won her trust without even buying a ticket in it, and when his interest in her was flat-out registering any higher than his waist.

Oh, yeah, no doubt about it! If there was a God, She was definitely female.

Prudence won through over Brett's ill-conceived idea to hang around the agency under the pretence of wanting to study the details of the London-based business Meaghan was so eager to purchase. There was no reason he couldn't review the prospectus at home, and a whole lot of reasons why waiting until Joanna finished work so he could drive her home wasn't a good idea. Not the least being that she *trusted* him, when merely hearing that soft, husky voice of hers say his name had him fantasising about what she'd sound like chanting it in the throes of passion.

A particularly fanciful image of desire-drowsy turquoise eyes watching him as he fanned silky jet hair over his pillow almost doubled him over as he crossed the lawn to the front door.

'This is getting ridiculous!' he snapped.

'Ah, and I do so prefer the sublime...'

The familiar but unexpected voice had Brett pivoting to see a six-foot-six giant walking up the path. 'Jason! G'day, mate. Great to see you!'

'Same here.' The reply was accompanied by a crushing bear hug and a macho thump on his shoulder. Brett gave an exaggerated grunt and forced a frown as they broke apart. 'You on a new weight regime?'

'Nah, it's just your time in the States turned you into a wuss,' his redheaded friend teased. 'Still, it's good to have you home. Life's too quiet when you're not around, McAlpine.'

'Yeah, right. You wouldn't know a quiet life if it bit you on the bum.'

'True, but I'd certainly be interested in getting better acquainted under those idyllic circumstances!'

Brett could only laugh. 'As incorrigible as ever, I see. When'd you get back?'

'About an hour ago. My cupboards are bare and the surf is flatter than a bowl of soup; so if there's no beer in your fridge it's really gonna crush me.'

'Don't sweat it, mate.' Brett motioned his lifetime friend up the front steps. 'A cold tinnie is as good as in your hand... But you only get one, before I take you to check out a place up at North Palm I've got my eye on.'

Jason stopped in his tracks, and, turning, raised a questioning eyebrow. 'What, you're home for good? How's Toni feel about that?'

'Yeah, I'm staying. And Toni, as they say in the classics, is history.'

'About time you came to your senses,' Jason muttered.

CHAPTER SEVEN

'OH! SORRY, Brett, I didn't realise you had guests.'

Joanna's arrival jerked his mind from the rough house plans he and Jason had spent the last few hours sketching.

'No! It's okay, Jo,' he said hastily, realising she was about to retreat. 'It's just Jason.'

'Who's not at all wounded by being dismissed as being so utterly unimportant,' his friend inserted. 'Anyone who's known Brettland as long as I have has learned to love him despite his appalling lack of manners.'

Brett would have liked to think Joanna's wide-eyed reaction was caused by his friend's warped sense of humour and high camp act, but he knew it wasn't. There was no disguising the rank amusement dancing in her eyes, despite the obvious struggle she was having keeping a grin at bay. *'Brettland?* Er…is that your real name?'

'Yeah,' he grunted. 'And the red-haired giant with the trout mouth is Jason Albridge.' He shot the man in question a lethal look, which typically he ignored, his attention on the room's latest arrival.

'Ah, you must be the charming Joanna I've heard so much about. Or does everyone call you Jo?'

'Er, no. Just Brett…sometimes.'

'Do I?' he asked, surprised by her comment.

She nodded. 'Just sometimes.'

'Oh.' He knew he *thought* of her as Jo, but since she was rarely wearing clothes in his head it seemed a bit personal to call her that in public. 'Sorry.'

'No, no! It's okay! I like it. That is, I don't mind.'

The idea that she'd noticed something he himself hadn't even been aware he was doing created a strange sensation within him. A gentler, less primal sensation than those she usually sparked, and it was an effort to drag his eyes from her and respond to whatever inane comment Jason was making. 'Huh?'

His friend merely shook his head. 'Forget it. It's obvious your interest in discussing house plans has suddenly plummeted to zero,' he said dryly. 'So I might as well head off home.'

To Brett that sounded like a great idea, as it meant he wouldn't be forced to try and concentrate on anything other than what he wanted to: Jo. Not that *she* gave a damn, he realised, hearing the next words out of her mouth.

'Why don't you stay for tea, Jason?'

'Tea?'

'I mean *dinner*. Sorry, I still slide into "bushie" speech occasionally.'

'Where exactly are you from?' he asked.

'A tiny town out in West Queensland. I doubt you've even heard of it.'

'Try me?' he challenged, oblivious to the way Brett was pointedly stacking up the work they'd been doing in the hope that he'd hurry up and go home.

'Kuttibark.'

Jason's face broke into a wide grin. In spontaneous response Joanna's lit with excitement. There was no mistaking her delight as she squealed, 'You know it!'

'Nope. Never heard of it!'

It was an old, hackneyed joke, but it had Joanna chortling with laughter and almost falling over herself insisting Jason *had* to stay for dinner.

Brett had to acknowledge that the resentment he felt over the guy's light-hearted flirting with Joanna wasn't a good sign. On a cerebral level he *knew* the force of the irritation he felt towards his friend was irrational, and that was all that stopped him from saying, *Hey, Jace, old buddy; remember you like your bread buttered on the other side.* If even his best friend, who was gay, could bring on the pangs of jealousy, then it pretty much indicated Brett's interest in Jo—*Joanna*—extended beyond that of a possible short-term, no strings relationship. Which was what Meaghan and he had feared and been tempted by respectively.

It was a realisation which both panicked him and had him wondering just how big a bastard he'd turned into that he could entertain ideas of a casual relationship with a woman as sweet, trusting and already emotionally scarred as Jo. *Joanna!* Jo-an-na! Damn it, he had to stop visualising her starkers! Right. And once he managed that he could start disciplining himself to ignore the way he felt when he looked up and found her watching him, and the way his body tightened when he watched her walk, or laugh, or just breathe.

'What are you groaning and muttering to yourself about?' Jason demanded. 'There's nothing wrong with sausages and boiled vegetables.'

'With gravy,' Joanna tacked on, which did little to clarify what the hell they were talking about.

'I like your ideas for the house,' she went on. 'But I don't understand why you don't want carpet. I always wished we'd had carpet.'

'In the West Queensland climate? You're kidding!' Despite his loathing of carpeting, on climatic, health and aesthetic grounds, he hadn't meant for his tone to come out sounding quite so scathing.

'I think it's better to lay carpet than to cut down valuable trees just so people can have fashionably polished floors,' she retorted. 'Using carpet also helps support the domestic wool industry,'

'Relax, Jo. The timber I use will come from plantations, not old growth forests,' he told her, fighting a smile at the evidence that she actually *did* read and absorb the information in the varied and copious quantities of magazines he'd noticed accumulating in the house. Then, remembering she did this to try and fill all the social and intellectual gaps of her childhood, his amusement faded to be replaced by a sensation so gentle he wanted only to hug her. Not jump on her in a frenzy of raw animal lust, just *hug* her and hold her and try to compensate for the crazy actions of her old man and the rest of her family.

By the time he'd crawled free of his thoughts, she was trying to haul a huge sack of potatoes out of the pantry and onto the sink-top.

'I've got it,' he said, moving instinctively to help her. His hands closed over hers, and as they did it felt as if every vital organ he possessed shut down.

He wasn't breathing—couldn't—yet the scent of her somehow managed to travel through his system. His blood was bubbling away at boiling point, but he remained frozen, bent over clutching her hands as they in turn clutched the tied neck of the sack of potatoes. When he lifted his head her face was only scant centimetres from his.

It was a face to make sculptors weep for its perfection.

Her vivid, almond-shaped eyes were wide open, but so still Brett felt certain he could dive into the crystal depths of those eyes and find his soul. He might have tried, had he not been distracted by the tip of a melon-pink tongue peeping nervously out from between lushly glossed lips. When it darted back out of sight the muscles in the pit of his belly felt as if they were being tightened by a winch. What would that mouth taste like...feel like beneath his? Would it transmit the serenity her fragile features suggested to soothe him, or match the passionate fire she ignited in him? And—

Without warning his hands were empty and she was out of his reach.

'It's okay, Brett,' he heard her say. 'I've spent my life lugging sacks three times the size of this. Third drawer, if you're looking for the potato peeler, Jason.'

'I was. You want the pumpkin peeled too?'

'Of course!' Her laughter warmed the room. 'You can't eat it with the skin on.'

'Rubbish! Butternut pumpkin baked in its skin is heaven...'

Though Brett heard, even comprehended every word of the inane ongoing banter between Joanna and Jason, he couldn't rally his thoughts enough to move beyond the sensory and emotional overload his body had just experienced and join in with some glib aside. He needed space and time to sort out what was happening to him. Somehow lust had got tangled with sentiment, and his most basic instincts were being dulled—or was it *sharpened*—by emotions usually reserved for those who *didn't* affect him on a sexual level.

His brain framed the excuse that he was going to have a shower before dinner, and the notion might or might not have been verbalised by his mouth; either way, he shut the pantry door and headed for the other half of the house.

Fifty minutes later, when he joined Jason and Joanna at the dinner table, it was with the relief of knowing he'd succeeded in getting things back into perspective. It had taken a bit of time to figure out, but ultimately he'd been able to chalk up his recent erratic emotions to the fact that he genuinely *liked* Joanna, and because of her youth and lack of experience in the real world he felt protective towards her. Which wouldn't normally have been a problem except that she was also excruciatingly attractive, naturally sensual, and his libido had unfortunately chosen now to start emerging from its hibernation of the last four months.

So, he'd come to the conclusion that it wasn't that he was any more physically attracted to Joanna than he would have been to any other beautiful, intelligent, sexy woman he might have encountered right now; it was just that the *non-sexual*, protective instincts she engendered in him were stronger than he'd have expected, and, taken by surprise, he'd got them muddled up with his need to get laid. Knowing the sooner he accomplished *that* the sooner he'd be back on an even keel, he found himself contemplating

Jason's invitation to attend an AIDS fund-raiser the following night.

If there'd been any one noticeable advantage in growing up having a sister, it was having been able to gain a valuable insight into how the female mind worked, and Brett's assessment was that: a) it invariably jumped to conclusions, which *always* put men in the wrong; b) it invariably jumped to the *wrong* conclusions, which *still* always managed to put men in the wrong; and c) the only time a woman *didn't* jump to conclusions was if doing so would work in a man's favour.

All of which meant that if he phoned any of his old girlfriends they'd wrongly assume he was interested in rekindling old passions and expect more than the one-night-only appeasement Brett was contemplating. The last thing he wanted to do was hurt the feelings of a woman he knew. Therefore the obvious solution was a one-night stand with someone whose current desire for commitment was as non-existent as his own. Though he'd prided himself on having outgrown the shallowness of casual sex, given the erotic ideas that watching Joanna spooning ice cream into her mouth inspired in him, it suddenly seemed like the most noble of sacrifices.

'So what about you, Brett?' Jason said, looking expectantly at him. 'Do you want to come tomorrow night or not?'

The unfortunately worded query had Brett choking on his own dessert. As he struggled to his feet, gasping, spluttering, his eyes tearing, Jo bounded out of her chair and hugged him from behind.

The sensation of having her breasts pressed hard against his back wasn't conducive to aiding his already oxygen-deprived lungs, although it was possible the vicious fist she slammed into his ribs—*twice*—might have been responsible for restarting his stalled heart. Survival instincts, however, kicked in, allowing him to catch her hand's third approach and pull her off him before she inflicted any more damage to both his nervous and skeletal system.

'Are...you try...ing to kill me?' he managed between coughs, eagerly accepting the glass of water Jason handed him.

'I didn't want you to choke to death.'

'So wh—?' He cleared his throat. 'What? You'd rather break my ribs and have me die of a punctured lung? Haven't you heard of patting someone on the back?'

Her expression was at best patronising. 'That's *not* what you do when someone's choking,' she told him. 'What I did is known as the Heimlich Manoeuvre, which is the *correct* way of dislodging obstacles from the air passages. I read about it in a magazine article on first aid.'

'Did they state a survival rate for the unfortunate victims subjected to this particular lifesaving technique?' he muttered, massaging his ribs.

'Never mind him, Joanna,' Jason told her, waiting until she'd resumed her chair before sitting down himself. 'Some people just don't know how to be grateful.'

She nodded, then gave a theatrical sigh. 'You're right. Next time I'll just let him choke.'

'Okay! I'm grateful! All right?' Brett knew he sounded anything but. Taking a calming breath, he tried to get past the fact that he was angry because in the space of a few seconds, due to something as innocuous as a spoonful of peaches and ice cream, Joanna had managed to again scramble his sensory circuit. It was pretty hard to credit that just *any* sexy, attractive woman trying to prevent him choking would have had the medically unprofessional effect on him she'd had.

'Let me rephrase that...' he said, refusing to tempt fate further and pushing his dessert aside. 'Thank you, Jo—er—Joanna! I appreciate your help.'

'That's okay. I only did it because I wanted to keep my record intact—I've never had anyone die eating a meal I've prepared yet.'

He told himself that her wink was intended to be cheeky, not suggestive. But while his brain bought that story his body didn't. He was damned grateful tomorrow night's charity do would provide a wall-to-wall choice of single, available socialites. Not that he was going to be too fussy. Right now, *'any port in a storm'* struck him as one hell of a handy motto to adopt!

He deliberately stayed in bed the next morning until he knew Joanna had left for work. He'd also been intending to hide out there when she got home from work until it was time for him to leave for the fund-raiser, but that idea bit the dust when she came charging into the house an hour earlier than she usually did.

'What are—?'

'Worked through my lunch hour,' she explained, somehow reading a mind which from where he was standing had blanked out at the sight of her. 'Haven't got time to talk now,' she added on a brief, bright smile as she darted past him down the hall.

Before he'd motivated himself to move from the spot where she'd left him standing, her head poked through the doorway of her room at the end of the hall. 'Can I *please* have the shower first?' she asked, her voice cajoling. 'I promise I won't be in there long.'

You would be if I joined you! He slapped down the thought. 'Go ahead,' he said wearily, telling himself that until he had a chance to placate his mutinous hormones tonight, the smart option was to avoid any discussion with her that might encroach on things even remotely sexual. 'Sing out when you're through, Jo—*anna*,' he added swiftly. 'I have to be out of here by six-thirty.'

He'd barely finished speaking when she burst back into the hallway. Raven hair flying about her shoulders, she used one hand to strategically clutch the front edges of an otherwise unsecured slinky robe and the other to carry a *huge* toiletry bag. A quick long-legged stride had her at the bathroom door in less than a heartbeat; not that *his* heart was still beating after the robe had parted to give him a brief, side-on view of one incredibly shapely limb from ankle to hip.

She paused at the door to shoot him a grateful smile. 'Thanks, Brett. You're an angel. I'll be quick; I promise.'

Then she slipped into the bathroom, leaving him pondering the paradoxical notion of how a guy could be angelic and horny simultaneously.

'Br-e-e-ett! Can you come here a minute?'

The urgent request came from down the hallway, just as he was pulling on his dinner jacket and anticipating a quick exit from the house.

Oh, God, what now?

'Brett!' she called again. 'Can you hear me?'

'Yeah, yeah. I can hear you,' he muttered. *Hear you, see you, smell you! Do every damn thing except touch you and get you out of my mind!*

He strode the short distance to her room, grateful that within a few minutes he'd be out of the house and taking the first step in a plan that would exorcise her from his brain.

'Yeah, wha—?'

Whatever he'd been intending to say wedged in his throat when he all but cannoned into the back of her in her doorway.

The predominantly *exposed* back of her.

Swallowing hard, twice, he shot out an arm to brace himself on the doorjamb as a defence against the erratic bouncing of a pulse which threatened to overpower what little balance was still keeping him upright.

The dress was black velvet, which, he decided, fighting to remain rational, was the only reason her skin looked so milky white. No human being could possibly have skin— so *much* skin—as white and soft-looking as hers appeared. And, dear Lord, he'd never known a woman could have a neck as beautiful as hers; his mouth was watering with the desire to taste it.

'Brett?' She frowned at him over her shoulder. 'Please…I need you to do me up. It's hard to reach and my nails are still wet.'

He swallowed again. 'Do what?'

'My *buttons*. Do up my buttons…'

She had to be kidding.

Do up her buttons! There were…*fourteen* of the damn things! Fourteen buttons running from the top of the high-collared creation along her spine to the deliciously tempting curve of her butt. Fourteen incy-wincy pearl buttons that needed to be pushed through a presumably corresponding number of loops. By him. He whose fingers, if they malfunctioned the way the rest of his body did when he got close enough for her perfume to corrupt his nervous system, would either become paralysed or start trembling…

There was no way he could do it without touching her. Uh-uh! *No way!*

'I can't do this.' Realising he'd spoken aloud, he added, 'Er, that is…can't you wait till your nails dry?'

Glancing over her shoulder, she studied him with a concerned frown. 'Brett…' Her tone was hesitant. 'Is something wrong? Have I…said or done something to upset you?'

'That'd depend on how you define the word "upset".' The sneered response caught them both unawares.

'Hang on!' he said quickly. 'That didn't come out the way it was supposed to. I didn't mean to snap.'

She stilled, but remained with her back to him. 'But I *have* done something to make you angry?'

Maybe if she hadn't sounded so confused, or if she'd substituted 'horny' for 'angry' he could have said yes. Instead, he exhaled every skerrick of breath in his lungs in the hope some of his tension would be expelled with it.

'No,' he said, forcing his fingers to the delicate pearl button and loop at the top of the high-necked dress, despite their wanton desire to start with the one at the base of her spine. 'I'm not angry at you. It's just that—'

He broke off when the first button slipped though the loop and his right thumb and index finger skimmed her skin. Gritting his teeth, he tried to imagine himself doing something totally gross. Nothing came to mind. It wasn't easy to conjure ugly thoughts when you where touching a living dream.

'Just that *what*?' she prodded.

'Huh? Oh, just that I'm under a lot of pressure at the moment.' *Ain't that the truth!*

'Because of Meaghan and her wanting to set up in London?' she enquired.

'Partly,' he said, deciding that since his sister had been responsible for putting him under the same roof as Jo she was more than entitled to wear some of the blame for his problems.

'Are you cold?' she asked.

Now *there* was something to wish for. 'No, that's one problem I don't have,' he said dryly, then drew a deep, steady breath. *Five down and nine to go.*

'It feels like your hands are shaking.'

Eight to go… 'They're not.' *Only a little white one.*

'Um…how long have you known Jason?'

'Since we were kids. His grandmother lived across the road and he moved in with her when his folks died.'

'How did it happen? How old was…?'

It was as if a fog settled around his senses about then, and when it finally receded he wasn't sure if he'd actually answered her questions or not. However, since he was vaguely aware of having heard his own voice merging with the husky melodious tones of hers, and since she was still standing trustingly in front of him, albeit squirming impatiently, presumably he'd said nothing untoward or suggestive to her.

His sigh was a combination of relief and dread. *Only four buttons left.* But these were really going to test his fortitude.

He paused and wiped his palms on his trousers before tackling them. It didn't help. Not when the already closed buttons had pulled the fabric snug to her body, enhancing her curves.

Once again clenching his teeth, he tried not to notice the tingle of awareness that travelled from her skin to the tips of his fingers and onwards through his entire body. Tried not to speculate about how she was going to get out of this thing tonight. Let's face it, about the only problem she'd face there was the high probability that if she called for volunteers to help her she'd never survive the stampede.

The gush of air he expelled when his fingers finally completed the task left him almost light-headed. It also alerted Joanna to the fact the task was completed.

'Thanks,' she said, moving quickly towards the walk-in wardrobe. 'I'll just grab my coat and we can go.'

'Excuse me?' He told himself that she couldn't have meant that the way he'd heard it. But he had a terrible feeling he was going to be wrong. 'Go where?'

'The supermarket.' She gave a half laugh. 'Where do you think? The fund-raiser, of course. Jason said...'

Brett was too busy cursing his friend to be interested in listening to anything he might have said. Damn! If he hadn't been so obsessed with trying *not* to think about her he might have managed to put two and two together and woken up to what was going on. *Now what was he supposed to do?* It was too late to bail out of the evening with just any excuse. And what about his plans for later tonight? What were his chances of finding a woman so desperate for an utterly meaningless night of passion that she'd view him having to bring Jo home as foreplay?

'Right!' she said, interrupting his thoughts. 'I'm ready.'

She emerged from the wardrobe with a cape of some description draped over her arm and a small purse in her hand.

All he could do was stare at her.

Since his own father had been a fashion designer Brett

had been immunised against the penchant some designers
had to shock. At least he hadn't been until right now.

Now he was not only shocked speechless, but *furious*.
He'd just sweated blood buttoning up the back of a dress
that gave the impression it was as chaste as a nun's habit,
only to discover the front had less material than the average
handkerchief! Oh, sure, it had a high collar, but from the
base of the neck it was dramatically slashed to show not
only every bit of cleavage Joanna possessed, but even a
teasing shadow of her navel. Adding a touch of bizarre,
ironic humour was a solitary loose string of faux pearls,
identical to the buttons so modestly securing the back; except these were draped to link both sides of the barely existing 'bodice' so that they swung against her breasts when
she moved.

It was a struggle to decide whether he was looking at his
ultimate dream or his worst nightmare. But when he finally
got his tongue unknotted from his tonsils the first words to
roll from his lips were terse.

'Put the coat on and let's get out of here.'

She frowned. 'I'm not sure I really need it... It doesn't
seem all that cold.'

'Joanna, for both our sakes... *Put...the...coat...on.*'

CHAPTER EIGHT

IF JOANNA ever needed extra cash fast Brett decided she could pick it up getting kickbacks from chiropractors; the instant she shed her coat most of the males in the cloak-room gave themselves whiplash.

'I didn't expect there to be so many people,' she confided as Brett halted at the entrance of the hotel's ballroom to scan the crowd. 'And everything is so elegant and sophisticated... I've never been anywhere like this before.'

Her naive excitement was so painfully at odds with her appearance Brett didn't know whether to laugh or cry.

'And thank heavens Jason told me to dress up.'

'Yeah,' Brett muttered, spotting what looked like his friend's flame-coloured hair and steering her in that direction. 'If you'd gone for anything *less* you'd have risked pneumonia.'

Their progress through the throng was made slow due to the number of old acquaintances who'd been unaware Brett was home and wanted instantly to start catching up on every detail of his life. Jo was charming to everyone, and with her Alice in Wonderland awe of her surroundings seemed oblivious to the appreciative glances her dress drew.

'Do you know *everyone* in Sydney?' she asked, when they finally escaped a prominent politician who, had she not had photographs or quotes in the papers twice a day, would have been subject to speculation that she was dead.

He shook his head. 'Not yet, but Mum does. Although, considering the attention you're drawing, I'll probably leave here having met every straight guy in the place.'

'*Straig*—oh!' She nodded with understanding.

As was typical at these functions, there was an assortment of socialites, politicians, actors, hospital board members and members of various gay organisations. Brett had been attending fund-raisers for AIDS research since the days when the number of people at a function like this would have been lucky to reach a hundred.

'Brett McAlpine! It's been *ages*! My God, it's *wonderful* to see you again! And goodness who's the princess in the daringly darling dress?'

Kirk O'Grady had never been one of Brett's favourite people. He was vain, malicious and utterly self-obsessed. If Toni was the disaster of *his* personal life, then Kirk held the same title in Jason's. For ten cents Brett would have knocked his pretty smile into the middle of next week. It took a real effort to be civil.

'Joanna, meet Kirk O'Grady. Kirk, Joanna Ford.'

'Joanna, sweetheart, it's delightful to meet you!' he gushed. 'And allow me to tell you your dress is absolutely dee-vine! A David Lingard, isn't it?'

Brett answered before Jo had time to recover from her embarrassment. 'Sorry, no kewpie doll, Kirk. It's a Nightwatch. Bye.' Snagging Jo's hand, he turned from the man and headed towards the bar.

'That was awfully rude,' she said.

'That's Kirk in a nutshell.'

'I meant the way you acted,' she clarified.

'Good. Let's hope he noticed.' At her murmur of surprise, he added, 'The guy's scum. A big-time user.'

She came to a dead stop. When he turned to see what was wrong, she stared at him in horrified amazement. 'As in *drugs*?'

He shook his head. 'Not as far as I know.'

When her frown remained, he continued to explain. 'I meant he's a user of *people*. Everything he does and says is aimed only at serving his own best interests. He's an emotionally crippled con-man who considers only himself as being important. If you get what I mean.'

Her eyes became rueful and chased all trace of the earlier joy from her face. 'Unfortunately, I do.' she said. 'I've had one of those people in my life.'

'Me too,' he admitted. 'Although fortunately Toni didn't mess me up as badly as Kirk did Jason. But,' he said, injecting a cheerful tone into his voice and giving her hand a reassuring squeeze, 'you'll get over What's-his-face.'

'What's-his—? Oh, right! Andrew.'

He grinned. 'See, you've practically forgotten him already! Now, what'll you have? Name your poison.'

Her expression went momentarily blank, then lightened with wry amusement. 'Okay,' she said, 'I'm going to presume that's some sort of slang, because while I admit What's-his-face—' she grinned '—left me feeling pretty sorry for myself, I'm passed the stage where I want to kill myself.'

Brett laughed. 'I'm asking you what you want to drink. You must find communicating with all those photographers and models a real challenge. At times even *I* think they have a language all their own.'

'Mmm,' she agreed. 'But I'm getting better at it. At least now I know that having a model tell me there's a guy in the building wanting to shoot her doesn't have me calling the police.'

'You *didn't*?'

Her dark head nodded. 'Unfortunately, I did.'

Brett's visual image of the scene had laughter rumbling in his chest.

Jo was grinning too. 'It's funny *now*, but at the time I thought I'd die of mortification *and* get fired. Thank heavens the model rang straight back and explained there'd been a mistake.'

'I bet you're still being given a hard time about that.' He opened his mouth to clarify the remark, but she jumped in before he got the chance.

'Yes. I still get *teased...*' she pulled a smug face

'...about it occasionally, but mostly it's good-natured. Just about everyone's been very nice and patient with me.'

'In my experience "nice" and "patient" aren't words most people associate with the modelling game,' he said dryly.

'Well... I guess I'd have to admit that for some reason the women aren't always as understanding as the men are...'

For some reason! Dear Lord, hadn't she ever looked in a mirror?

'I think the reason you're looking for is fear of the competition,' he informed her.

For several seconds she actually stood there as if the comment warranted consideration, before firmly shaking her head—an action which caused the pearls at her breasts to start swinging. *Damn!* And he'd been doing so well at keeping his gaze locked above her neck!

A drink! He needed a drink! Fast.

If he'd been thinking clearly he'd have taken her straight to the table and *then* returned to get the drinks. But because he'd been reluctant to leave her alone in a dress which could conceivably start a riot, he now had her pressed to his side by a crowd of people all wanting to quench their thirst.

'Geez, you'd think the organisers would've anticipated this and provided the tables with drink waiters!'

A middle-aged woman in front of him turned to scowl at him. 'Sir, there will be drink waiters during the meal,' she said, indicating he'd spoken his frustration aloud. 'We had hoped people would appreciate that by keeping catering overheads to a minimum we'll have more money to donate to the research facilities.'

When she turned away without waiting for a response, Joanna giggled. An action which caused her body to vibrate against his, sending sparks of awareness showering through him. Then, as if that wasn't enough to steam his senses, she linked her arm through his and rose on her toes to say in a confidential tone, 'In case you didn't notice, you've just had your knuckles rapped.'

Big deal. If *she* got any closer someone could whip out a knife and start performing open heart surgery on him and he wouldn't notice!

'By the way,' she said. 'When you asked me to name my poison was that a trick question?'

'A trick question?' he echoed, having no idea of what she was talking about, but totally fascinated by the mouth that had produced the words.

'Yes, a test.'

The only test Brett was aware of was the one of strength going on inside him, between his hormones and his brain. And, Lord, he hoped his hormones won!

'To see if I remembered your lecture on how to...' she grinned '...avoid being *slipped a mickey*?'

Almost rendered completely brain-dead by the intent way she was gazing up him, it took him an age to grasp what she was talking about. When he finally did, he could no more have prevented his finger from stroking the smooth, youthful skin of her cheek than he could stifle the growth of the soft, warm heat filling his chest.

'No, Jo, it's not a test. Tonight you can have anything you want.' His fantasy was that she'd reply with, *I want you*.

'Anything, huh?'

The teasing, flirtatious grin raised hopes he *knew* didn't stand a chance, yet he couldn't prevent himself from holding his breath in anticipation as he nodded.

'In that case,' she drawled, 'I think I'd like to try something I haven't had before...'

Oh, God, me too!

'I think I'll have a Grasshopper.'

Brett went from holding the hopes of a prince back to feeling like a toad.

'Brett,' she whispered anxiously, her breath grazing his ear. 'Help me...' A hand shook his knee. 'I can't remember which fork I'm supposed to use.'

Fork! She'd just sent a thousand volts ripping through his body, leaving him grateful just to be able to remember his own name, and she was fretting over a *fork*? Why was it he couldn't generate one shred of interest in the blonde on his right, who'd spent the entrée practically in his lap, yet something as simple as a whispered request for an etiquette update and a kneecap nudge from Jo could send him into meltdown?

'Brett...' This time the whisper was accompanied with a not so gentle elbow to the ribs. 'Help m—'

The dinner conversation was sufficiently loud to shield her startled gasp as he grabbed her hand under the table. He'd acted purely with the intention of discreetly guiding it to the correct fork, but now that he held it he didn't want to let her go.

The decision, though, was quite literally taken out of his hands when she snatched it away. That she wasn't happy with his behaviour was more than evident in the turquoise glare she sent him. *'What are you doing?'* she whispered.

'Trying to *discreetly* show you the right for—' Her foot hit his ankle. Hard.

'Don't shout,' she muttered out of the side of her mouth.

'I'm not shouting.'

'Then don't talk.' With a bright smile she said something to the guy at the end of the table before again frowning at Brett. 'Just let me get a better look at the one you're using.'

His first impulse was to snap, *Work it out for yourself!* but that would have been childish and unwarranted. The guy on her left had spent most of the meal trying to keep Jason's attention.

'The outside one,' he finally muttered.

'Thank you.'

'Any time.'

Determinedly he turned his attention back to his right.

By the end of the night he would be fascinated by this blonde or dead from trying!

Later he told himself the only reason the blonde had diverted her attentions elsewhere was because he'd ignored her attempts at chit-chat during the address by one of the world's foremost authorities on AIDS research. Now Natasha, or Natalia, or whatever the hell she'd said her name was, was draped over some guy on the dance floor. Unfortunately not the one who, a few feet from her, was draping himself over Jo.

'All in all it's been a damned successful night, don't you think?'

The question drifted to Brett from the small group of people who were gathered at the end of the table chatting to Jason. In his own mind, while he imagined the organisers had raised a pretty respectable sum from the evening, in terms of personal success he figured he'd have had better luck trying to surf in the Antarc—

His self-pity stalled at the sight of Jo trying to convince her dance partner she wasn't interested in an encore. Though she was smiling, her head was shaking very emphatically, and she was trying to tug her wrist from the Neanderthal's grasp.

In an instant he was out of his chair.

'I wondered where you got to,' he said, as he reached her side.

'Brett!'

There was something incredibly heady in the welcoming way she said his name. A part of him refused to accept his brain's insistence that it stemmed only from the relief of being rescued.

'Er…Brett, this is Peter,' she said. 'Peter, Brett McAlpine.'

The polite introduction was wasted since Peter didn't even bother to lift his eyes from the front of Jo's dress long enough to enable him ever to recognise him again. Which, Brett decided, would be a plus if he had to go in a police line-up for punching the jerk's face through the back of his head. However, because he couldn't count on all the potential eye witnesses to testify to temporary blindness, he very reluctantly pursued a less aggressive and far less satisfying tactic.

'I believe,' he said, taking Joanna's arm and drawing her to him, 'that this is my dance.'

'Hey! Back off, mate! I'm not finished yet. A man deserves some reward for having to put up with a bunch of bores all night!' Heads turned as the inebriated man's insult carried.

Brett only had the luxury of grabbing the front of the guy's shirt and jerking him forward before two impeccably dressed men appeared from nowhere to flank them. Brett recognised them as professional bouncers and friends of Jason's.

'Problem, Brett?' the smaller man asked. His slight European accent triggered recall of his name.

'Yeah, Stefan,' he said, making no attempt to lower the drunk from his toes. 'You guys got here too fast. My knuckles are still itching.'

'Sir.' The second bouncer addressed the drunk in a commendably respectful tone under the circumstances. 'I think it might be time for you to leave.'

After appearing to be searching his inebriated brain for another insult, much to Brett's disappointment he changed his microscopic mind and meekly nodded.

'Um…Brett…' the taller guy said, his voice deep and amused. 'You're going to have to let him go.'

He did so, with sufficient enthusiasm to cause the guy to stagger backwards. Fighting grins, the bouncers grabbed the guy's elbows to steady him. Their grips, Brett noted with satisfaction, *more* than tight enough to thwart the attempts to shrug them away.

'Are you all right?' he asked, scanning Joanna's face for signs of distress but seeing only bemusement.

'I think so,' she said uncertainly.

'If you want, we could leave.' The offer had her looking aghast.

'*Leave?* Heavens, no!'

'Are you certain?'

'Yes—'

'Don't feel you have to be polite.'

'I'm not—'

'If you want to go home, say so. Because I really don't mind.'

'*Brett!* I…don't…want…to…go…home.'

It wasn't the insistence in her voice that stemmed his words, but the fact she'd clamped her hands on his forearms to ensure his attention. Unfortunately, once she realised her action, she quickly let him go.

They stood facing each other on the perimeter of the dance floor. To the left, people were chatting in groups and wandering in and out of the now sparsely populated tables. To their right, couples were dancing in semi-darkness to a Billy Joel song, and for the first time in his life Brett didn't know what to say or do next.

Joanna Ford was the most puzzling, fascinating woman he'd ever encountered. She looked and dressed like a siren, yet she possessed a vulnerability and innocence that made her seem as if she belonged in another century. At times she got him so hot and bothered his sole urge was to find the nearest flat surface and make love to her until they were both unconscious; at others her naivety either drove him crazy or so enchanted him it produced the most overwhelming need to cherish and protect her.

Brett understood none of it. He'd believed his upbringing and having a twin sister had provided him with a far better insight into women than most men, but Joanna Ford had him completely bamboozled.

She was a twenty-two-year-old whose experience of life was negligible. He was a financially secure thirty-four-year-old who'd lived on every continent before he was twenty. Hell, there probably weren't enough years in her future for her to experience everything he'd done in his past! Yet from the minute he saw her she'd tied him in knots, and ever since had been tugging those invisible strings tighter and tighter.

'Dance with me.' The words came from him of their own accord.

'I...' She darted a nervous glance towards the now crowded dance floor, then looked back to him. 'I'm not very good at it. I'll probably embarrass you.'

Giving her no time to think, he pulled her into his arms and began to weave into the throng.

'The good news is,' he said, forcing himself to hold her in a discreet waltz position they'd been taught at school, 'I don't embarrass easily. The bad news—'

She winced, and faltered.

Instinctively he pulled her closer.

Tilting her head back, she met his gaze. 'I take it,' she said, humour tugging at her mouth, *'that's* the bad news,'

He sighed. 'Yeah. Sorry. You want to sit down?'

'Do you?'

Let her out of his arms? She had to be kidding!

'No,' he said. 'But then you're not trampling all over *my* feet.'

'You're not that bad. You've only done it once.'

'Maybe, but I think you should know the last woman I danced with was my deb partner. I hear she's still wearing orthopaedic shoes.'

He felt her soft laugh vibrate all the way to his soul.

'Oh, that's nothing,' she told him, her turquoise eyes bright. 'The last man *I* danced with could barely stand up and had to be helped away by two fully grown men.'

Brett laughed. 'And I thought it was because he was drunk.'

He felt the heavy hand land on his shoulder at the same instant Jo's face lit up in an elated smile. 'Steve Cooper! What are you doing here?'

'Hoping to get a dance with you? Mind if I cut in, mate?'

Hell, yes, Brett minded! *Who the devil was this guy?*

Jo read his mind. 'This is Steve Cooper—'

He'd guessed that much already! But what was he to Jo?

It wasn't until Cooper frowned that Brett realised he was ignoring the guy's outstretched hand. It was more reflex than good manners that eventually had him shaking it. He was also blaming good manners for the fact that the next thing he knew he was making his way back through the throng to his table and Jo was tripping the light fan-bloody-tastic with some guy who looked as if he bench-pressed Mack trucks for a living!

Brett turned instantly at the sound of her voice to find her hurrying across the room as fast as the narrow, sexy black velvet dress would let her. He grinned to himself. Cooper might have got to dance with her for the last hour and a half, but it was a one-man field as to who was going to be around to undo those fourteen little pearl buttons when she got home.

'You ready to leave?' he asked when she reached him.

'Yes. But I wanted to know if you'd mind if I asked Steve back to the house for coffee? It's just so great to meet someone from my past! And we've got so much catching up to do.'

Past! What past? She'd had a repressed upbringing in some unheard of minuscule country town! And the only time she'd tried to escape it she'd been taken for a ride by some married jerk called Andrew! After that she'd high-tailed it to Sydney and to the best of his knowledge had been under his sister's protective wing ever since. So where did this Cooper fit in to her so-called *past*?

'Jo,' he said, in a painstakingly reasonable tone, his fists clenched in his pockets, 'you're more than welcome to invite guests to the house. However, do you think Stan—?'

'Steve.'

'Right. Do you think he really wants to drive *all the way*

up to Whale Beach at this time of night? It's a good fifty-minute drive one way.'

'That's what *he* said.' She sighed.

Brett fought down a smug grin.

'Oh, well…' She shrugged, wearing a resigned smile. 'I guess we'll just do what he suggested and stay the night at his grandmother's place.'

CHAPTER NINE

ARRIVING at the pub fifteen minutes before he was due to meet his cousin, Glen, Brett made his way through the eclectic Saturday afternoon crowd to the bar and ordered a beer. In summer the air-conditioned coolness of the beach-side pub was a haven for sun-burned surfers from the heat; in winter it was equally popular as a venue to watch football or horse-racing on the big-screen TV. His cousin's suggestion they meet here and spend a while 'catching up' before Brett joined him and his family for dinner had worked out well. After four hours spent listening to the hard sell of assorted real-estate agents, Brett was ready for some down-time, and the informal ambience of the pub suited him just fine…

At least it did until he turned from the bar and encountered the heart-stopping smile of a raven-haired angel.

'Hi,' she beamed. 'What are you doing here?'

The question, an echo of the one which had flashed through his mind, albeit behind, *Where the hell have you been all day?* would have been *his* opening line had he not been distracted by her snug, but flesh-concealing sweater. While the change of clothes indicated she'd *finally* gone home at some stage today, it also refreshed Brett's nagging curiosity as to where she'd been and how'd she'd got out of the dress she'd worn last night. A thought which immediately had him ignoring her question and scanning the nearby area for that Cooper guy she'd gone home with.

'Brett…'

'I'm meeting someone.' The ridiculous, light-headed relief he felt at not seeing the man anywhere made it easier to answer her question than to try and formulate an intelligent one of his own; he sure as hell couldn't ask what she and Cooper had got up to last night while they were at his grandmother's! He realised she didn't necessarily have to be here with him, but in the absence of *any* apparent competition hovering nearby Brett wasn't about to waste time asking for answers he didn't want to hear.

When her puzzled expression made him realise he'd been grinning at her like an idiot for several silent seconds, he said the first thing that popped into his head. 'I'm supposed to meet my cousin, but I'm early.'

She nodded, then turned her smile down a few thousand watts as she swung it to the barman and ordered an OJ. 'In that case,' she said, 'if you've got a few minutes could you help me out with something?'

He wondered if she'd used that same appealing tone to coerce Cooper into undoing the buttons on her dress—*yeah, right!* Like any guy with a pulse would've needed to be coerced into *that*!

'What?' he asked, more sharply than he'd intended, paying for her drink before she could get her fingers in and out of the pocket of her impossibly tight jeans.

'Thanks.'

'I haven't said I'd help you yet.'

She grinned. 'I meant for the drink.'

Dismissing her gratitude with a shrug, he guided her towards a small high table with two vacant bar stools. 'These seats okay?'

She nodded. 'Yeah, we'll get a good view of the TV.'

The only thing Brett wanted a good view of was her. The closer the better; for as long as possible. And, as much as he'd been looking forward to seeing Glen, he started fervently hoping his cousin, a renowned punctuality freak, pulled a flat tyre on his way here so he'd have more time with Jo. The chances of her being here alone were slim to nothing, but he'd take what he could get; he sure wasn't about to jog her memory of who might be waiting for her by opening a conversation by asking how she came to be here. But nor could he casually ask what she'd done today, since that would also eventually lead her to the same reply; so for what seemed a decade they sat in a tension-laden silence in a pub bustling with noise.

'It's nice here,' she said eventually. 'Er…do you come here often?'

He raised a teasing eyebrow. 'Not a very original pick-up line, Jo. It's the female version of "What's-a-nice-girl-like-you-doing-in-a-place-like-this?" *Which*, you'll notice, I've refrained from asking.'

She groaned and rolled her eyes. 'I was being *serious*. Besides,' she added, her expression coy, 'my opening line was to say hello and ask for a favour; it can't have been too bad because you've already bought me a drink.'

'Then I guess we're at stage two…'

'I guess so.'

Her elegant hands nervously grabbed at her water-beaded glass and she took a sip of juice through the straw. There was an air of uncertain reticence in her actions which intensified Brett's feeling that what she was preparing to ask him was something she considered personal, something that would affect his opinion of her. Perhaps alter the current footing of their relationship. Though he fought down the temptation to let either his imagination or libido second-guess her, he couldn't help thinking, *No hard feelings, Glen, mate, but two flat tyres would be a godsend for me about now.*

'So, what is it you want to ask me, Jo?'

A shy blush rose in her cheeks, but her exotic eyes lit with an excitement that could only be labelled illicit.

'This will probably shock you,' she cautioned. 'And it's totally out of character for me to be considering this…but I know what I'm doing. I mean, doing it once doesn't mean I won't be able to control my impulses in future.'

Brett felt his hopes, not to mention other parts of his anatomy, bolstered fractionally, but he could hardly blame them. She was gazing intently into his eyes, and keeping a lid on his emotions wasn't made any easier by the way she leaned close to him with an intimacy suggesting her words shouldn't be heard by anyone's ears but his.

'I want you to—' she whispered, then broke off, glancing away.

His throat tightened in anticipation. 'You want me to *what*?' His voice was scratchy and uneven, and he was torn between watching the battle between uncertainty and resolution on her face and the rise and fall of her breast as she took a deep breath.

'I…I want you to put a bet on a horse for me. I want to try gambling.'

Brett waited for disappointment to kill him. It didn't. It did, however, make him feel fifty kinds of fool. And then some. Afraid he'd incriminate himself if he tried to verbalise his feelings, he took a long, settling swallow of beer.

'Except,' she said, 'I don't know how to do it. Would you show me how to do it?'

He took another, longer swallow.

'The horse I want to back is called Lust 'n' Laughter.'

Brett drained the glass. And just barely refrained from taking a bite out of it and gulping that down too.

She wanted to bet on a horse. A horse called Lust 'n' Laughter, of all things! He didn't know whether to laugh, cry or immediately have himself neutered. Then again, given the way his mind, *and body*, seemed to assimilate everything on a sensual level whenever he got within sight of this woman, the latter was probably the best option. *Where the hell was Glen?*

'I've already got a TAB ticket.' She shifted on her stool to pull it from the back pocket of her jeans. 'But I didn't know how to fill it in. Until I saw you I was going to ask the barman to help me.'

Oh, great, the poor bloke behind the bar was sixty if he was a day; he'd have probably had a stroke from the excitement if she'd phrased her proposal to him the way she had to Brett.

Scrambling to get beyond the stupidity of his frustration, and the frustration of his stupidity, he took the ticket and looked at it. 'You want to take a quinella?'

'What's a quinella?'

He sighed. 'It's when you pick the horses that will finish first and second.'

'But I don't want to pick two horses. I only like Lust 'n' Laughter.'

Brett gritted his teeth as irony again hit him with a sucker punch. 'Then you need a different ticket.'

'Okay, I'll go get—'

He clamped a hand on her arm when she would have bolted from the table. 'Stay put. I'll do it.' *And get myself another drink while I'm at it,* he added silently, a desperate glance at the entrance revealing no sign of his cousin. Terrific. Of all the times for him to break the habit of a lifetime and be late!

'How much do you want to bet, and do you want to bet it each way or only for a win?' His question produced total bewilderment on Jo's beautiful face.

'What's the difference?'

'Each way,' he said, with forced patience, 'means you'll collect money even if the horse finishes second or third. If you just back it for a win and it only gets a place you get nothing.'

'Oh, each way, then!' she said. 'Definitely each way. There might be a faster horse in the race.'

A dry laugh broke from him and he pointed to one of the small TV sets suspended above the bar. 'Since your choice is showing at thirty-three to one, I'd say there's a good chance of that. I'm not much of a gambler, but even I know that in a seven-horse field odds like that aren't a good sign. Sure you don't want to pick something else?'

Emphatically shaking her head, she wriggled around until she could prise some change from her pocket, then shoved a two-dollar coin at him. The idea of watching her repeat the seductive squirming which producing the small coin had required tempted Brett to urge her to increase the minuscule wager, but, not confident his blood pressure would take it, he simply palmed the money and headed to the section of the bar where the tote computer was installed.

'Oh, thank heavens!' she exclaimed, when he made his way back to the table. 'I was wondering where you'd got to. The race is about to start.'

'Sorry. I got a beer then decided I better check the other bars in case my cousin was waiting in one of them. It's not like him to be late for—'

'Hey! This ticket is for *four* dollars, not two.'

'Half of it's mine.' He shrugged. 'I figured if you've got a hot tip, I don't want to miss out on it.'

Genuine concern clouded her face. 'But, Brett, what if it loses? I don't want to be responsible for you losing your money.'

'Jo...it's *two* dollars; trust me, I can spare it.'

'Still, I—'

'And they've jumped in...'

Whatever protest she'd been going to make was forgotten as her eyes flew to the big screen. The race was a distance of fifteen hundred metres, but Brett didn't see the field of horses cover even one of those; he was too transfixed by the rapt pleasure and anticipation in Jo's face and her ability to surrender herself completely to her emotions.

She started out perched on the edge of her stool, whispering, 'Go, Lust 'n' Laughter.' Then progressed to standing, clench-fisted, with her even white teeth nibbling on her bottom lip. Watching her interest develop from mere excitement to a point where she was jumping up and down cheering the horse's name was both a revealing and disturbing experience for Brett. It made him wonder how hard she'd had to work to subdue her instinctive enthusiasm for the little things in life in order to survive her family's rigid view of it. It also had him speculating on just how unfettered and passionate a lover she'd be.

By the time the horses hit the home straight, Jo's was

making a late run from the tail of the field down the outside, and she was pumping her arms and chanting, 'C'mon! *C'mon!* Go, Lusty, *go!*' When it managed to stagger over the line to grab third place, she cheered as if she was the owner of a horse that had just won the Melbourne Cup.

'We won! We won!' she screamed. Laughing with undiluted joy, she threw her arms around Brett and kissed his cheek. The action so stunned him that she'd danced out of his reach before he could do anything more than freeze in shock. Although how that was possible when his body felt as if it had been hit with a zillion volts of electricity was beyond him.

'Oh, Brett, we won!' she continued to enthuse, unconcerned by the amused looks she was drawing as she danced around the table waving the ticket. 'We won!'

'Er...actually, Jo,' he said, through a chuckle, 'we only got *third.*'

She waved a dismissing hand. 'Same thing! Oh, wait till I go tell Steve! He told me I was throwing my money away!'

The words iced Brett's veins. 'Steve's *here*?'

'Mmm. He's in the other bar playing in a pool competition. Too boring for me. I—'

'Brett! Mate, I'm so sorry I'm late. I—'

'On the contrary, Glen,' he muttered. 'Your timing is perfect. Spot-on, in fact. Here, let me introduce you to my punting partner.'

He waited until Jo and Glen had finished uttering polite greetings to each other, then said, 'Well, I'll leave you to collect the winnings, Jo. And if you want to make any more bets you're going to have to get your *date* to do it. Glen and I have to be going.'

'*Already?*' Glen protested. 'I haven't even had a beer yet.'

'Yeah, well, we'll buy a slab in the bottle shop on the way to your place. See ya, Jo.'

'Er...okay. Um, bye. And, er...thanks. I'll see you at

home, then. Nice meeting you, Glen.' She gave a limp-fingered wave, wearing the expression of someone who'd walked into a movie late, couldn't make head or tail of what was happening but wasn't going to admit it. Glen wasn't that reticent.

'What the hell is going on?' he demanded, following Brett's rapid exit to the car park. 'I thought the plan was we were going to have a few light beers before we went to my place.'

'We would've, if you hadn't chosen today out of an entire lifetime to be late. The way I'm feeling right now, if we stick around here any longer I'm likely to make an idiot of myself by breaking a pool cue over someone's head.'

Glen laughed. 'Yeah, right! You'd be the last person in the world to get into a pub brawl.'

'I used to think you'd be the last person in the world not to be somewhere on time too, but it happened,' Brett muttered.

'Fair go, mate, I never expected to have a flat on the car...'

CHAPTER TEN

IT WAS two weeks before Brett learned who and what Steve Cooper was, and then only by chance, since he'd vowed not to ask Joanna even if it choked him. In fact, after the weekend of the fund-raiser and the encounter at the pub, he'd done a good job of if not putting her out of his mind, then at least keeping out of her way. Not that it was all that hard when she was out practically every night of the week and had anything up to six things going on over the weekend. Still, the up-side of all the Joanna-free time was that his business and professional future was moving ahead at full speed.

After discussion with five television networks he'd narrowed the choice of which one to link with down to two. He was now in the comfortable position of merely fielding the bids and counter-bids as they fought each other with offers of impressive salary packages to secure his services. He'd also commenced negotiations with the owners of three mid-market home furnishing stores with the possibility of him buying into the business and expanding it on a national scale. So far the financially secure but commercially short-sighted threesome were still too bemused to really talk turkey. However, Brett was prepared to give them a few months to come to terms with his ideas before giving them a further nudge. One of them had already shown definite signs of interest...

As for his personal life...well, if there was one thing cohabiting with Jo had shown him it was that he had to get out *fast*! Even limited contact with her was putting him under more mental and hormonal stress than even a saint could handle! If she didn't stop breezing into the living room clad only in a slinky robe to sprawl out on the sofa either to paint her nails or flick through magazines while he was trying to watch the late news or sports... Well, he was going to have to kill one of them. If he spent any more time hiding out at Jason's place, his friend was going to start demanding rent!

So, his first inclination when he heard her come in the front door late on a Thursday night was to bid her a brief hello and adjourn to his bedroom, before she had a chance to start telling him about her day. Before her husky voice and delighted smile made him wish he'd been there to witness first-hand the pleasure she got from everyday things most people took for granted.

Last night she'd come in bubbling over the fact Steve had taken her to a small travelling fairground. She'd laughingly admitted that she'd been so terrified for the first fifteen seconds on the ferris wheel that she'd thought she was going to be sick, but then she'd opened her eyes and '...*I was so close to the stars I felt I could just reach out and pluck one from the sky.*'

None of the women Brett knew would have admitted to such feelings even if they'd had them, but Jo shared her joy as if she couldn't imagine others hadn't felt the same way. Although Brett had discovered this charming quality had a vicious edge. Her description of her first taste of candy floss had been so damned sensual he'd been almost suicidal at not being the one responsible for introducing her to it.

'Hi,' she said, pausing at the entrance of the living room and holding carry-bags bearing the names of various shoe and clothing stores.

'Been late-night shopping, I see,' he said, trying to keep his gaze casual even as the sight of her kicked his pulse up several gears.

'Reluctantly,' she moaned. She moved wearily to dump the bags on the nearby sofa and perch on the arm. 'Meaghan wouldn't take no for an answer. She's so excited about going to London and checking out the agency there I think she's running on jet fuel and assumes everyone else is too.

'If we didn't go to every designer boutique in the city,' she went on, her eyes bright with good humour, 'it was only because they were closed. I'm convinced she's the marathon champion of shopping. I ache from head to foot.'

'Nah, that's just a light sprint session for Meaghan,' Brett teased. 'When she's in marathon-mode she hits the suburban stores as well. You must be out of condition.'

'Don't you start.' She scowled. 'I've been told that enough by Steve. Believe me, *his* idea of keeping things light differs from mine.'

'Keeping *what* light?' Brett demanded, jealousy spurring him to his feet.

Her expression suggested the answer should be obvious. 'My workouts, of course.'

'Your *workouts*?'

She nodded. 'He's a personal fitness trainer. He's been helping me to get into shape and tone up.'

Brett made a long, slow visual appraisal of the woman separated from him by a coffee table and two metres of floor space. Loose tresses of jet hair tumbled onto her shoulders from a fashionably untidy topknot. A boat-necked black angora dress displayed a long neck and just a hint of clavicle, then stretched down to embrace the ideally rounded curves of her breast and hips before revealing twelve inches of black nylon-clad legs.

Tonight there were no long boots shielding them, and Brett felt his body tighten in appreciation of her chunky shoes. *Yeah, right, he'd always had a fetish for ugly-looking shoes!*

Finally, in an act of sympathy for his hormones, he forced his eyes back up to hers.

'Jo, if you think there's the slightest thing wrong with your tone or shape,' he said gruffly, 'you're as crazy as

Cooper. You need a personal fitness trainer like the Sahara needs more sand.'

She blushed and offered a self-conscious thank you. Then said, 'I think Steve just offered to let me use his gym because he felt sorry for me at school.'

If Jo believed *that* she was even more naive than he'd originally feared, or she'd never seen a mirror. But his curiosity was snagged by the school concept, because he'd estimated Cooper as being in his late twenties—at least five years older than Jo.

'You went through school with this guy?'

She shook her head. 'He was one of the sport masters the year I was at boarding school,' she clarified. 'Sport was compulsory for live-in students, but because my parents had never allowed me to take part in it at my other school I was pretty hopeless. Actually, I didn't even know how to swim,' she admitted, her head dipping sheepishly for a moment.

'Anyway,' she continued, 'when Steve found out he volunteered to give me private coaching and arranged with the principal for me to have access to one lane of the school pool twice a day when the swim squad were training. Then, when I could swim four hundred metres without stopping, he took me to the beach so I could learn to handle rougher conditions.' Her face broke into a radiant smile. 'I'd never seen a beach before then.'

'Nice guy,' Brett muttered, hating him for it.

'*Very,*' she agreed, bending to regather up her shopping bags. 'And I'm glad he's found another career; all us girls in the dorm always thought he was too nice to be a teacher!'

And too damn good-looking! Brett added silently, wondering what idiot had employed him to work in a private girls' school.

'If you haven't eaten, there's some left-over stir-fry in the refrigerator,' he said as she started from the room.

She paused and looked over her shoulder, wincing slightly as she did so. 'Thanks, but much as I love all the exotic meals you cook, I think I need a long hot soak in a bath first.'

For the next forty minutes Brett sat in front of the TV telling himself he *needed* to keep abreast of the latest scientific breakthroughs in the treatment of ticks in cattle—it was easier than admitting he was waiting for her to come in search of food just so he could catch one last glimpse of her before he went to bed. Oh, God! he thought, flinging his head back against the couch and contemplating the ceiling. Had he ever been this emotionally wired in his entire life before?

'Oh, good, you're still up...'

His heart leapt out of his chest at the sound of her voice. It was soft, light and sensual. He swallowed. So was the peach-coloured negligée she wore. It was also frilly and painfully short.

'So you do own something that isn't black.' The comment probably struck her as inane, but it gave him a good excuse for the way his eyes refused to budge from her. He searched and found another one to do the same.

'You know, Jo, with your eyes you'd look dynamite in turquoise. Black is such a cliché.'

'Maybe to you,' she said. 'But for me it's liberating. I was always forbidden to wear black. Besides, I've read several articles that have said black goes anywhere.'

'Although presumably not to bed.'

Her shrug not only sent ripples of awareness through his belly, but lifted the swell of her creamy breast above the scooped neckline of frills. He fought down a groan of frustration, unsure if his mind was playing tricks on his tortured body or if he could see the dark peaks of her breasts beneath the two layers of gossamer fabric.

'Actually,' she said, gliding over to perch on the arm of his chair, 'I bought this in a moment of weakness when I was on my way to deposit my wages in the bank. I really didn't need it, and it was criminally expensive,' she confessed. 'But it was too pretty to resist.' She sighed heavily.

'I think I need to stop deliberately blocking out my father's lectures on the evils of giving in to temptation, or I might find myself in trouble if my credit card application is approved.'

Brett figured that he and temptation were already shaking hands! If he didn't get out of here fast, he was going to forget that she was a young, naive girl who'd already been taken advantage of by one guy and, as Meaghan had pointed out, was still vulnerable.

Ultimately, though, it was the memory of Jo's own admission that she trusted him which propelled him to his feet. 'Right. Well, I'm off to bed—'

'No, wait. Here.' She snagged his hand and pressed a metal bottle into it.

Presumably she'd been holding it when she entered the room, but since her hands hadn't been the focal point of his interest he hadn't noted it. He did now. 'Goanna Oil?'

'Steve swears it's the best thing for sore muscles. The school swim team used it all the time.'

'Yes? So? Why does he think I need it?'

She laughed. 'It's not for *you*, you goose! It's for *me*. I want you to rub it on my back. I—'

The metal clanged hard against his mother's imported Italian tiles.

Bounced once. Twice. Then eventually rolled under the coffee table.

'Oops! Sorry. I thought you had hold of it,' Jo apologised, scampering to retrieve it.

Brett remained catatonic.

'Oh, thank heaven it didn't spill!' she said, presenting her beautifully rounded butt to him as she knelt to reach the bottle. 'We'd have had oil all over the place!'

'You want me to massage your back?'

She sighed. *'Desperately.* I started doing some weight work the day before yesterday; now I'm really starting to get achy and stiff. You know what it's like...'

Oh, yeah, he knew!

'The day after you don't really notice it, but the second day...' Groaning, she sat back on her haunches and began to flex her shoulder. 'Boy, that's when it starts to *kill*!'

'Er, don't you think you'd be better off having a hot shower or—?'

'Tried that. It hasn't helped.' Her expression became beseeching. 'Please, Brett? I phoned Steve and he said a rub down with this would help.'

I just bet he did!

'Please,' she cajoled. 'It's only got to be a quick one.'

Her choice of words didn't help the situation one iota! Temptation squeezed Brett like a vice. *What the devil had he done in his past life to deserve such torture in this one?*

'I wouldn't ask if I wasn't in agony.'

'Yeah, okay! Okay! I'll do it.' *God help me!* 'Lie down.'

Her face flooded with pleasure. 'Oh, thank you! So where do you want to do it? On my bed—?'

'No!'

Her astounded reaction to his snarled response didn't do anything to improve his mood. Good! Maybe if he could stay furious, he just might get through the next few minutes without embarrassing either her or himself.

'Er...well, then, where do you want me to lie?'

Under me! His mind screamed.

'The floor!' his mouth snapped. 'On that rug over there! Hurry up and get comfortable. I'll be back in a minute.'

Storming into the adjoining room, he made a beeline to the bar, uncapped the first bottle his hand fell on and took three long gulps. Lowering it from his mouth, he blinked his watering eyes and studied the label. Russian vodka. Hell, if that couldn't get him through this ordeal nothing could!

He'd expected her skin to be soft, yet the texture of it beneath his fingers as they trailed the length of her arms made him think of whipped cream. A ridiculously whimsical notion, but one that projected such highly erotic images it caused his heart to double shuffle and the heat in his groin to burn hotter. She was hot, too. He could feel the heat in her skin...

With a whimpered mew, she turned to him.

Oh, yeah...she was hot, too. The evidence was in the liquid arousal in her eyes, the raspy shallow breaths she drew and the way her nipples pressed hard against the cool rich fabric of her gown. The temptation they offered was too much for his mouth to resist; lowering his head, he tongued one through the fabric. The feminine half-gasp, half-whimper made him smile. Oh, yeah...she was hot all right. Hot for *him* and ready to be loved to the point of meltdown. His and hers.

The force of her hands grabbing his head in a desperate bid to bring his mouth to hers commanded he oblige, but when the taste of her moans threatened to strip him of his control he forced her from him. He wanted to possess her more than he'd ever wanted to possess any woman, but he wanted it his way. She'd already messed up his mind and tortured his libido enough, he reminded himself.

Stepping back, he slowly began to unbutton his shirt. When she reached to assist he increased the distance between them.

'Uh-uh, babe,' he whispered. 'I want you to see what you're getting.' He didn't care that the words sounded egotistical; he loved watching the way her eyes devoured him, the way she now pressed her palms flat against the wall as if it was taking every ounce of her control not to jump his bones.

The thought almost made him surrender. Damn, but she was the only woman who'd ever made him hot and horny just by looking at him. And the hell of it was she didn't know it. He wanted her to know it. He wanted her to know that she could flick his switch with just one slow, lazy look from those eyes of hers. He wanted her to know so that the knowledge could turn her on at times when it was utterly impossible for her to do anything but let her insides burn with unsatisfied lust.

He discarded the shirt and reached for her hand. It was elegantly fragile and small within his, and though it trembled it cupped his erection with a confidence which caught him off guard. The surge of his blood made him dizzy, but it was nothing compared to the sensations which assaulted his senses when she bent and licked a criss-cross pattern over his chest. Yet when her languid tongue trekked its way between each of his ribs and down the furred centre of his belly to his navel, his legs came so close to buckling he had to grab *her* for support, his fingers driving through her raven hair to anchor against her skull.

She disposed of his belt and both his trousers and jocks with a competence that surprised him and a smile sufficiently smug to restore his need for control. Snaring her wrists before her hands could entrap his now bare shaft, he stepped out of his pants and kicked them aside.

Meeting her excited gaze with a deliberately lazy one, he walked her backwards the three small steps it took to sandwich her between him and the wall. The scent of her perfume drifted around them like smoke. Her pupils were dilated with raw, uncut desire. Her breasts rose and sank against the gossamer silk still shielding her body from his eyes. But it wasn't a shield against *his* body. Keeping his gaze locked on hers, he rubbed against the coolness of the fabric and felt his blood catch fire from the heat radiating from beneath it. Her heat.

When she started to ride against him the loud, throaty moan of arousal that cut the darkness might have belonged to either or both of them as their mouths fused in primal hunger. Her hands and nails pressed into his buttocks with an impatience that granted permission for him to take her with speed and begged him to do it *now*. He rose above the temptation, knowing he'd find far greater pleasure in pleasuring her.

So he worked to calm her with soft kisses and whispered

words. With feather-light caresses of her arms, shoulders and throat. Then, when she was lulled to soft whimpers that begged for him, *only him...all of him*, he slowly began to ease the now warm silk up her legs.

The delicate lingerie was a torment to his eyes and an erotic distraction for his fingers, but it was the delicate heated flesh beneath it which had him cramping with desire and caused his passion to bead in anticipation. Still nothing could have prepared him for the overwhelming surge of lust that tore through his body when his hand encountered no barrier to her feminine core. Her hot, slick and *oh, so ready feminine core.*

He told himself to go slowly, but she bucked once, hard, against his hand, and he needed no second invitation.

Never had he felt so utterly male as he watched her fling back her head, chanting his name as her nails dug into his shoulders and she frenetically rode his fingers. Never had his own control been so challenged, so tenuous he feared he wouldn't last long enough to find complete enjoyment in what he literally held in his hand.

In his head he heard a crash of metal, and her scream lift above it, but the clang continued to echo dimly in his head—

Brett woke with a jolt and instinctively reached for where Joanna—*wasn't lying*. The bed was cold.

It took his hormone-drunk brain less than a second to realise that he was alone in the tangle of black satin sheets. That his tortured mind had been the victim of a dream. The kind he'd long ago outgrown!

Disbelief warred with anger and self-disgust as he turned the darkness of his room blue with a string of apt and heart-felt expletives. He sprang from the bed, furious with himself, but more furious with the raven-haired witch who'd invaded almost every minute of his waking day and now had the audacity to encroach on his sleep as well!

Muttering under his breath, he snatched up the bathrobe

which her presence in the house necessitated and strode into the hall with the intention of taking a shower. The glow from the kitchen light altered his plans and he turned in that direction, cinching the belt of the robe tight enough to rupture his spleen.

The sight which greeted him was as bemusing as it was explanatory.

The presence of several saucepans and their assorted lids scattered across the slate floor accounted for the cymbal-like clang which had woken him. It didn't, however, explain what Joanna was doing in the faint dawn light covered from head to foot in flour!

CHAPTER ELEVEN

'WHAT the hell are you doing?'

She jumped at the sound of his voice, then glanced down at the unholy mess surrounding her. 'Would you believe *cooking*?' she asked, producing a cute, sheepish smile.

Brett wasn't amused. Not least because she was clad in the negligée of the night before. Irony had never been so cruel, nor so frustrating.

'A friend I know is having a…a party tonight,' she explained, the break in her voice indicating she wasn't oblivious to his mood. 'I promised I'd bring a cake and I wanted to make it before I went to work.'

'Well, couldn't you have done it quietly?' he barked. 'Or, better yet, considering the mess you're making, just *bought* a cake on your way home? Hell, the way you dress it's not like you've got to rely on your culinary skills to impress *men*!'

Brett regretted his tone and choice of words even before her face fell with shock and hurt. He couldn't have felt any worse if he'd slapped her.

'Jo, I'm sorry!' he said quickly. 'I swear I didn't mean that the way it sounded.'

Straightening her back, she eased back onto her heels, one flour-dusted hand unsteady as it slipped a strand of hair behind her ear.

'There's no need to apologise,' she said, with obviously forced dignity. 'My own sister has said far worse to me.'

Brett dropped to his knees in front of her and grasped her hands. 'Jo, please…I didn't mean that.'

Her turquoise eyes were shiny with threatening tears. 'You mightn't have meant to say it, Brett. But if the thought hadn't been somewhere in your head to start with it couldn't have come out.'

He had no doubt she'd read that in some magazine article, but did she have to be so damn serene and rational? Why wasn't she ranting and raving, or grabbing the nearest saucepan and hitting him over the head? God knew, he deserved that and more.

'Jo, listen to me a minute,' he urged.

She shook her head. 'I don't have time. I need to clean this up before I go to work. I'm sorry I woke you...' She pulled free of his hands. 'Go back to bed and let—'

'I'm not going anywhere until we straighten this out,' he told her.

'I made the mess; I'll clean it.'

'I'm not talking about the damned kitchen, and you know it!' He clamped a hand on her thigh, only to deter her attempts to stand, but her recoil from his touch was like a kick to guts.

Last night when he'd massaged her shoulders, he'd had to force himself to block out the purrs of pleasure she'd emitted as she'd begun to relax. How he'd resisted the temptation of really making her moan was something which had kept him awake most of the night. When he finally *had* managed sleep, he'd taken her in his dreams. Now, within moments of waking, he'd managed to insult and alienate her for no reason other than his own frustration.

Raking his hair, he tried to find the words to atone for his stupidity, but came up empty. In the end he decided to tell her the truth, or as near as he could get to it without giving the impression he was a sex-starved lunatic who was rapidly becoming obsessed with her.

Oh, God, how pathetically accurate was *that* description!

This time when she would've risen, he resorted to words. 'Please, Jo, hear me out... You know I wouldn't deliberately hurt you.'

'No, I don't know that.' Her voice was low and her head was bent, studying her hands. 'You're virtually a stranger to me. And I was wrong in thinking my own sister would never deliberately hurt me.'

'You told me you trusted me,' he said. 'How can you trust me if you think I'd want to hurt you?'

'Th-that's different. Besides, I don't mean you'd physically hurt me.'

He wanted to tell her that, no, he wouldn't hurt her physically, but that still didn't stop him wanting to make an assault on her body in an entirely different way. He'd have been no less honest in telling her that he so regretted what he'd said that his chest ached and his stomach was churning. Except his pain didn't come entirely from guilt; some came from the gut fear that if he didn't sort this out now, Joanna would be packing her bags.

'Jo, will you just hear me out? *Please?*'

He got no response or acknowledgement that she'd even heard him. But since she made no effort to move away he took this as a positive sign.

'The thing is...' he started, addressing the raven crown of her bent head, but paused to study the ethereal effect the now rising sun had on its satin smoothness. Even when he was scrambling to save his sorry skin, she was a distraction and a fascination he couldn't ignore...

He tried again. 'Jo... My head is in a hell of a mess right now. For personal *and* professional reasons.' It was the truth; ambiguous, but the truth nonetheless. 'The fact, is the person I was really angry with this morning was myself. This...' he indicated the mess that surrounded them '...and you... Well, unfortunately they just gave me a handy outlet for that anger.

'It was easier to be angry with the situation than it was myself. External problems are less threatening than internal ones.'

'That doesn't explain your snide comment about the way I dress,' she told him, lifting her head to look him squarely in the eyes. 'I can understand you being angry about being woken at the crack of dawn and finding this disaster, but what you said was really personal.'

He couldn't deny it. Nor could he tell her that *she* was the source of his problems and that they all revolved around sexual fantasies. Chances were that even if at some point in her bid to self-educate herself on life she *had* managed to scan an article on the subject, she wasn't going to be flattered by such an admission. This was a girl still wholesome enough to get a thrill out of receiving a three-dollar pair of chopsticks and candy floss.

When he emerged from his musing it was to find her watching him with a mixture of curiosity, disgust and disappointment. It was enough to spur him to speech.

'Okay, I admit the comment I made probably subconsciously stemmed from a problem I have with the way you dress, but I didn't mean it the way you think,' he said. 'I wasn't implying you were cheap. And it's *my* problem. Not yours.'

He wondered where she'd learned to look so sceptical.

'The thing is, Jo, you're an incredibly beautiful woman, but in my opinion you tend to slightly overstate things when it comes to your clothes. That's not to say you dress badly,' he hastened to add. 'You've got a flair for fashion and an excellent eye for quality. You also know how to co-ordinate—'

'Oh, and that takes *real* flair when I only wear black,' she piped up.

The underlying amusement in her sarcasm had him scanning her face to see if he'd imagined it. The faint almost-smile nudging her lips was enough to send relief flooding through him.

'Go on,' she urged. 'Now tell me what I'm doing wrong.'

It wasn't an in-your-face challenge, but her words had a definite you're-not-getting-off-the-hook-that-easily inflection.

'And I want the truth,' she added, seeming to know he'd been contemplating soft-pedalling her.

'All right,' he agreed.

'Well, for starters,' he said, 'the truth is you'd look brilliant in anything...'

'*But?*' she prodded.

'But...by opting exclusively for unrelieved black and dramatic, avant-garde styles you aren't really doing yourself any favours. Sure, people *look* at you, but they don't really *see* you; the clothes become the first and last thing they remember. Now that's what designers want from catwalk models, but Dad always said he got more joy out of seeing a woman wearing one of his creations than seeing one of his outfits *wearing the woman*.

'I'm not saying you should play it safe all the time,' he told her. 'Merely suggesting you vary your wardrobe a little so that when you *do* go for the dramatic people will say, "Doesn't Joanna look fabulous"; rather than "Doesn't Joanna's *outfit* look fabulous."'

She looked so intent, Brett wasn't sure whether she was contemplating what he'd said, still trying to absorb it, or if the concept had escaped her completely. She frowned questioningly as she said, 'In other words I should work on the "less is more" theory?'

He grinned his approval. 'More succinctly put than my effort and spot-on. *Except*, perhaps,' he added, 'in the case of the dress you wore to the fund-raiser the other night. If there'd been any less of that you'd have been arrested.'

She flushed. 'It was *that* bad?'

Brett sighed and forced himself to be objective. No, the dress hadn't been *that* bad. His problems with it had started before he'd been aware of its daring neckline. They'd started even before his trembling fingers had buttoned her into it and continued escalating from there. He'd boiled with jealousy at every admiring male gaze fired in her direction and now, two weeks later, he was still ready to punch walls every time he thought of Steve Cooper undoing the buttons on it later that evening.

There wasn't really anything wrong with the dress; just his mind.

'No, it wasn't that bad, Jo,' he said finally. 'In fact it was a stunning dress. You looked fantastic in it.'

Her pleasure at the words was evident.

'The thing is, Jo, don't think you have to work hard to look great. With your face and figure it doesn't matter what you wear.'

'It does to me.'

'Well, yes, I understand that—'

'No, you don't, Brett,' she said softly. 'Not really.' She sighed. 'I spent all my childhood being made to wear clothes that the parents of other children wouldn't have dreamed of putting their children in, let alone sent them out in public wearing them. Oh, they weren't old,' she qualified. 'Mother sewed me three new dresses every year—sometimes more if I had a growth spurt. But they were always plain and ugly and all based on childish styles of the fifties.'

Once again Brett could only imagine how difficult her life must have been; he and Meaghan had been the ones to *set* fashion trends amongst their peers.

'So fashionable clothes were another "sin" to your family?'

She nodded. 'That was one of the reasons I enjoyed my time at boarding school so much; uniforms were compulsory, and for the first time in my life I wasn't obviously different to other girls my age.

'I'd never *worn* much less owned a pair of jeans until Andrew bought me a pair. I know now they were only the chainstore variety, but to me they were the most fabulous gift anyone had ever given me. As much as he hurt and humiliated me, I'll probably always think kindly of him for that.

'My sister Faith told me I'm cheap, shallow and vain, but...' Her breasts rose and fell as she took two steadying breaths, but on this occasion the action didn't stir Brett on a sexual level, but somewhere much deeper.

'Honey…' He reached out and gently cupped her face. 'A person's most honest, genuine beliefs are those they form themselves, not those they have forced down their throat. You're none of those things your sister said.'

She bit her lip and eased back from his touch. 'Thank you.'

'I don't want your gratitude, Jo. I'd rather hear you swear to forgive me for acting like a jerk this morning.'

Her mouth curved into a smile. 'Sorry, but I was brought up not to swear or blaspheme. I might've rejected most of my family's beliefs, but I've never thought that a particularly unreasonable one.'

Brett mentally cringed at the countless times he must have offended her with his own uncensored dialogue.

'But if you're genuinely contrite and looking for a penance you could always make a pot of tea while I get started cleaning up,' she teased, scampering to her feet. 'I'm not certain it'll impress God all that much, but…' she winked '…it'll definitely get you back in my good books.'

Five hours later Brett drove into the underground parking lot of the agency for yet another meeting with Meaghan and a plethora of legal eagles about the proposed purchase of the UK firm. But that wasn't what was occupying his mind.

He was convinced the brawl-and-bond session in the kitchen that morning was a positive step in the relationship between him and Joanna. He wasn't certain why he felt this, but suspected it was because for once they'd stopped tiptoeing around and being so stiltedly polite and considering of the other. Well, at least that was what *he* felt as if he'd been doing since he'd come home three weeks—

Was it really only that long? Geez, it seemed as if he'd been living on his nerves, or more accurately his hormones, for three centuries! Which proved that not only was trying to pretend he wasn't attracted to Jo dishonest, but stress-inducing. At thirty-four he should begin trying to eliminate stress from his life, not cultivate it.

Which left him where? he asked himself, activating the car alarm and crossing to the elevators.

Well, for starters, telling his compulsively maternal, paranoid sister that all bets were off! Sure, Jo was young, but she was six years beyond gaol-bait and she *had* had a lover. And, while she might be a novice when it came to the flash, glitter and grime of the real world, she had a strength and emotional maturity beyond her years. She hadn't rebelled against her background out of wilfulness, but rather from a genuine belief that she didn't belong there.

She recounted incidents from her miserable childhood without ever bad-mouthing or showing resentment towards her parents, though in his opinion such actions would have been justified, and despite the way her sister had disowned her after the fiasco with the married creep Jo still wrote to her. He realised then that he'd never once heard her say a bad word against *anyone*. Hell, she was still grateful to her mongrel of an ex-boyfriend for giving her a pair of jeans!

He took out the irritation that thought produced by viciously stabbing the 'DOOR CLOSE' button of the elevator and the floor number.

Sure she lacked the street smarts and superfluous social graces of most of her contemporaries, but she was also devoid of their jaded cynicism. She was intelligent, articulate and ambitious, though thankfully not obsessively so. Her sense of humour was delightful and she possessed an insatiable curiosity and, as their trip to the cave had shown, a dash of daring.

The bottom line here, Brett realised with no great surprise, was that Joanna Ford fascinated him and he'd end up a wreck if he didn't stop pretending otherwise and do something about it! It was time he got off the sideline and into the game, and gave Steve-wonder-coach-Cooper a little competition!

In fact, it was way past time! So, while Cooper might have a date for tonight with her, there was no time like the present to start running a little interference.

He was still smirking with self-satisfaction when the elevator doors slid open at his designated floor and brought him face to face with his sister.

'What are you grinning like an idiot about?'

'Just the fact that I'm through acting like one.'

Meaghan smiled and nodded. 'Thanks for pointing that out. I'd hate to hurt your feelings by not noticing it.'

Stepping back and rising onto her toes to kiss his cheek, she let the elevator leave without her. 'I also hate to ruin your obvious good mood by telling you this...but you're too early. The meeting isn't scheduled for another hour.'

'No problem,' he replied easily. 'I'm here to take Jo to lunch.'

'Oh? Then in that case I'm afraid you *do* have a problem.'

Brett fought to keep his voice even. 'Meaghan...look, you're my sister and I love you dearly, but I am *not* going to make a martyr of myself for your noble causes, regardless of how well-intentioned your motives may be.'

'Okay,' she conceded with a breezy shrug. 'But you're still not going to be having lunch with Joanna... She's left for the day.'

'Left! When? How long ago?'

'Brett...this might come as a surprise to you, but I'm too busy to stand at the front door and keep a log of when my staff come and go. Since she asked to leave at twelve-thirty, I assume that's when she left.'

Brett glanced at his watch. Damn! He'd missed her by thirteen minutes. Then again... 'Catch you later, Meaghan!' he said. 'If I don't make the meeting...have it without me!'

'If—Brett!' she yelled as he hurried down the corridor. 'You better make the meeting; I need you there!'

'Rubbish! In case you haven't noticed, you've been running this place solo for four years. You'll handle it on your ear,' he assured her, knowing his presence at the previous meetings had been superfluous. Giving her a thumbs-up sign, he turned and darted in the direction of the reception area at a fast jog. Fortunately, aided by his leather-soled shoes and the tiled lobby, a radical shift of his weight was all that was necessary to avoid colliding with two slow-moving models and have him literally skating into the reception desk. The thud of his hands acting as brakes on the timber gained him the instant attention of the two people sitting behind it.

'Brett!' Elation burst through him at the sight of Jo's startled and startling face. 'Is something wrong?'

'Not now I've found you.' He grinned at her wide-eyed reaction to his deliberately silky tone. 'I came to take you out for a slap-up Chinese lunch.'

'Half her luck,' the girl next to her purred, her pouty smile lost on Brett.

'Oh…well, thanks…' Faint pink tinged Jo's cheeks. 'That's very nice of you, Brett. But I'm using some of my accrued flexi-time and taking the afternoon off. I was planning on just grabbing a hamburger and doing shopping.'

He shrugged. 'Okay, I'm easy. A hamburger and shopping is cool with me. You about ready to leave?'

She blinked. 'Er, well…yes, but… Don't you have a meeting scheduled?'

'Not any more.'

'So what are we shopping for after burgers?' he asked five minutes later as he guided her out of the building and across the road to a fast food shop.

'Well, first I want to stop by the bank and pick up my credit card.' She grinned. 'They rang this morning saying my application had been approved.'

Brett grimaced theatrically. 'Ahh. And like all women you're so eager to give it some exercise you're going to spend the afternoon buying stuff that in all likelihood you don't need.'

'No, I'm going to buy stuff I *do* need, but didn't know I needed until you told me.' She laughed, undoubtedly at the baffled expression Brett knew he had to be wearing. '*Clothes*, Brett... I'm buying some "understated" clothes, that aren't *black*."

Partly from the guilt he felt for being indirectly responsible for Joanna going into possible debt splashing out on new clothes, but mostly because he wanted to impress her, Brett insisted he knew just the place for her to shop.

As they drove through the congested traffic of the once blue-collar, now fashionably upmarket suburb of Rozelle into the neighbouring and even more trendy area of Balmain, he could feel Joanna watching him with such scorching intensity he felt as if he was on fire. No, more likely it was his own desire burning away at him, he decided later, when it managed to destroy his concentration to the point where he almost missed his turn. Making it late, he found the nose of the car mere metres from two jaywalking, grunge era leftovers who were either blind or had a death wish. Jumping hard on the brakes, he brought the car to a timely, but body-jarring halt.

Blowing out a relieved breath, he turned to Jo. 'Sorry about that.'

She started, as if not expecting to see him in the driver's seat. 'Uh...about what?'

'Never mind,' he said, amused by her vagueness. 'Mentally calculating exactly how you're going to dent the plastic, huh?'

'Calculating what?' Her confusion was so gorgeous he couldn't decide whether it would be a good or bad thing were she ever to be totally demystified by slang.

'How you're going to spend your money,' he amended, cruising the street slowly and scanning for a parking spot. *Bingo!*

'Oh, I see. No, I wasn't doing that. Well, in a way I was,' she corrected herself. 'I was wondering if it hurt much when you got your ear pierced.'

'Why? Thinking of having yours done?'

'Oh, I've already decided I'm definitely getting that done today,' she told him. 'But I'm still uncertain about getting my navel done.'

The thump that shook his body could have been his heart, but since even when shocked it didn't normally sound like crushing metal Brett had a horrible feeling he'd just had the first prang of his driving career. The ashen face of his passenger pretty much confirmed it.

'Joanna…are you all right?'

She nodded.

'You're sure?'

'Yes, yes, I'm fine. Are you all right?'

'Never mind me,' he told her, gently taking her chin. 'How's your neck?'

'Brett!' She jerked her head away. 'My neck's fine. Okay? You were only reverse parking. You barely nudged it.'

He knew she was right, but it didn't dull his irritation any. Did she have to react so negatively every time he touched her? How was it she could be willing to let him rub oil over her back, when she was practically naked from the waist up, but every other time he touched her she acted as if he had bubonic plague!

Sighing, he got out of the car and walked fatalistically to the rear of it.

Unlike Meaghan, for seventeen years he'd had a flawless driving history. Now, within a four-hundred-metre distance he'd narrowly missed wiping out two pedestrians and managed to dent his mother's car. While he wasn't going to cast blame on anyone but himself, the woman in the passenger seat had definitely been a contributing factor to both incidents. The health department should slap a sticker on her stating: *Warning! This woman can affect your mental*

*and physical reactions—do not drive, or operate heavy or
dangerous machinery while in her presence.*

'Oh, that doesn't look too serious at all,' Jo said with
cheerful relief when she joined him at the rear of the car.

'I doubt the panelbeater's invoice will reflect that assessment,' he muttered.

Physically his mother's car had come out the worst of it,
but the 'victim', a black, customised Mercedes Sports with
a paint job that looked as if gold plating would've come
cheaper, was going to run to a nice hefty sum and wouldn't
please the insurance company. He bent to inspect the extent
of the damage underneath and noted the registration plate.
The very distinctive car had equally distinctive vanity
plates: *Carlo 7.*

'Brett!'

He straightened at the panic in Jo's voice and immediately sighted the source. A very large, very excited Italian
was running towards him, waving his arms and shouting,
'Mamma mia! I cannota believe this!'

Before Brett could do or say anything, he was seized by
the rotund middle-aged man.

CHAPTER TWELVE

CARLO BIORDI had been nicknamed 'The Italian Bear' by a very young Meaghan because of his overpowering welcoming embraces and his equally bear-like bulk. Nothing had changed, and Brett was once again subjected to fervent hugs and air kisses, punctuated with chants of, 'Ah, my young Brett! It's a binna too, too long! Mucha, mucha too long!'

As his father's old friend patted him on the back with close to violent enthusiasm, Joanna stood back looking more than a little bewildered. No doubt she'd been anticipating the owner of the car attacking him with anger, not unchecked joy. Brett winked at her over Carlo's shoulder. 'It's okay. I think I've met him once before.'

When Carlo finally wound down, he stepped back and made a thorough head-to-toe inspection of Brett. '*Si*, you are Mac's son!' he stated approvingly.

'Mum'll be glad to know you verified that for her.'

Carlo chuckled. 'She's in Europe, no?'

'She is, if it's August.'

'And her health; she's well?'

'Fighting fit. Still trying to foist her business onto Meaghan or me, of course, but so far we've been able to palm her off. With luck she'll start directing her efforts towards Karessa real soon.'

'Ah, the *bambina*! She's getting big, no?'

Brett nodded. 'Fourteen last birthday.'

'*Mamma mia!* The years go too quick. Too quick!' he insisted. After a moment of pensive head-shaking, he said, 'So tella me this, Brett, why after four years have you come to wrecka my beautiful car, uh?'

Brett smiled sheepishly. 'Yeah, I'm sorry about that, Carlo. I got distracted for a second and… Well, I think the damage is severe enough that the insurance companies might want a police report. I'll give them a call now.'

'Pah! Forget the police! We deal with this bit of nothing later! But now we talk! Be sociable! Come inside.'

'Well, actually, Carlo, I'm here for business purposes—'

The old man's face lit up like a Christmas tree. 'Atta last! Ah, Mac and the angels musta be celebrating witha the Chianti!'

Brett raised a silencing hand. 'Don't get too excited, Carlo. My foray into the fashion industry is extremely short-term. And I'm afraid on the most minuscule scale. I've merely brought you a potential new client.'

He gently turned the man in Joanna's direction.

'Carlo, I'd like you to meet Joanna Ford; Joanna, Carlo Biordi—fashion designer extraordinaire and my late father's closest and dearest friend…and, as you've just witnessed, forgiving to a fault when someone creams his latest luxury toy.'

They spent over three hours with Carlo, and Brett enjoyed every minute of it. Once Joanna had ceased insisting she couldn't afford anything but off-the-rack clothes, she'd given in to Carlo's demands that she tell him the sort of clothes she wanted. Carlo, of course, had very firm opinions on how 'such fragile beauty shoulda be presented.' But in no time he and Joanna were engaged in an animated and excited exchange of ideas. Not since his father died had Brett sat and watched anyone sketch the most detailed of creations from nothing but the vaguest description.

Bar a few occasions when he was required to translate some of the designer's Italian-English for Jo, Brett's presence was virtually redundant. When they eventually left it was with promises from Carlo that he would start making the patterns immediately and would call Joanna soon.

The next stop Jo wanted to make was at a jewellery store

to have her ears pierced. Fortunately, a large sign stated the staff did not pierce any other parts of the anatomy. They left the store with her grinning like a kid at Christmas and insisting that despite her winces and watery eyes at the time, the stud gun hadn't hurt a bit!

Finally she had him stop at a patisserie so she could purchase an extremely decadent chocolate and coffee confection to take to her party. For Brett it was a signal that the hours he'd enjoyed basking in her bubbly laughter and chatter were drawing to an end, and for most of the trip home he felt wired and edgy.

By the time they reached home, he'd decided sitting around while she got ready for a date with another man was too masochistic to endure, and he headed straight for the surf. But nature wasn't feeling any empathy for him and he returned to the house after less than an hour when a late afternoon wind shift made conditions more frustrating than challenging.

He was about to walk into the laundry to shed his wetsuit when mutterings in the kitchen had him detouring to find Jo seated at the table rummaging through the open first aid kit.

'Joanna…'

She turned, and the sight of her tearstained face had him negating the distance between them without his feet touching the floor, his heart pressing against his teeth.

'Honey, what happened? Where are you hurt?' he asked, scanning for blood as he crouched next to her chair. 'Should I get a doctor?'

'I don't need a doctor.' Her forehead creased with annoyance. 'I'm not hurt. Just useless.' She hooked her hair behind her right ear and turned her head so he could inspect it.

He hissed at the inflamed lobe. 'What happened?'

'I took the stud out, so—'

'Why the devil did you do that?'

'*Because,*' she said testily, 'I wanted to wear the gypsy hoops I bought.'

'Jo,' he said, 'the saleswoman told you the studs had to stay in at least four weeks.'

'No, she didn't. She said I had to keep *earrings* in continually for four weeks. She didn't specify it had to be *these*.' She dropped the offending item on the table and began reading the instructions on a tube of antiseptic cream.

'This sounds like it might help,' she mused aloud, but Brett didn't respond.

Now that he knew she wasn't in any danger of bleeding to death or passing out, it was impossible to ignore the fact that this self-induced calamity had befallen her between showering and selecting what she would wear. Her unsecured robe hung open and over the sides of her chair, drawing attention to rather than concealing the white camisole and matching pair of high-cut French knickers she wore beneath it.

Her blood might not have been flowing unchecked, but right now Brett's was heating so fast his wetsuit was probably about to melt onto his skin.

'I wish now I *had* had my navel pierced.'

The grumbled words lured his eyes to her belly and the deep dimple peeking out between the hem of her camisole and the vee front of her panties. The image of a stone the same colour as her eyes somehow affixed there made Brett's knees almost buckle, but the thought of that perfect milky skin being marred by a needle was enough to banish the idea.

'I think…' He stopped to clear the desire from his throat. 'I think the chances of getting an infection in your navel might be higher than getting one in your ear.'

'Who cares? At least I'd be able to *see* where to thread the earring!'

Her testy tone stunned him, before surprise gave way to amusement. '*Finally!*' he said with exaggerated relief. 'Evidence that you aren't always the paragon of patience and acceptance you appear.'

'Oh, I get annoyed about things,' she said. 'But I try not to let them get the better of me.'

'*Annoyed*, but never steaming, ranting and raving angry?'

'Not really…' Her tone was pensive. 'I've always found it quicker and simpler just to *shoot* the offender. Eeek!'

Her yelp of surprise and giggles resulted from Brett grabbing her wrists and tugging her out of the chair.

'Has anyone ever told you,' he asked, 'that you're too cute for your own good?'

Laughing, she shook her head and went to pull free. Brett's hands tightened of their own accord, his thumbs stroking across the inside of her wrist. With his own pulse vibrating through his body he couldn't detect hers, but the playful amusement which had been in her face was now replaced by something more intent.

Her eyes were dreamy soft as they lifted to his. Then, as he stood too mesmerised to look away from the serenity of her beauty, their turquoise depths darkened to a smoky teal. The transformation was spellbinding. No, *she* was spellbinding.

'Do you know what colour your eyes are?' Considering it was a ridiculous question, it seemed to take an age for her to answer.

'They're…blue.'

He shook his head. 'Turquoise. They're a true turquoise. Exactly the same colour as the stones in my bangle.' Though he'd unwittingly increased the pressure of his right hand against her wrist, as if to draw it to her attention, he was thrilled when she didn't respond and her eyes remained locked on his.

'But they aren't turquoise now, Jo,' he said, hearing the awe echo in his words. 'They've darkened to a deep, glorious—

'Teal…' he finished feebly, trying to work out how his hands had become empty and why Jo was across the room opening the freezer. He didn't put much stock in the bizarrely hopeful notion that she kept a supply of condoms there.

'T-teal, huh? Interesting…'

She didn't sound interested.

'But I read that it's quite a common occurrence for people's eyes to change colour. Apparently some people—'

He shut his ears to her trivial explanation. The only person's eyes he wanted to talk about were hers. And the effect they had on him. How could she not have felt the…the soft, sensual energy which had enveloped them a few moments ago? His own lungs had been frozen by the experience. Surely something that powerful couldn't be all one-sided. Dear Lord, a moment ago he'd looked in her eyes and would have sworn they shared the same thoughts, the same wants and the same *needs*; that all those emotions he'd felt were flowing on an endless three-sixty-degree circuit from his soul into hers and back again.

Damn it, had she read something that would explain *that* to him?

Brett didn't know how long she'd been chattering on without him hearing anything but his own inner confusion, yet typically he chose the wrong time to tune back into her.

'Anyway, I better hurry and finish getting dressed. Steve's going to be here shortly and…'

He managed to keep his succinct four-letter expletive trapped behind his clenched teeth, but containing the desire to put his fists through the wall of toughened glass was proving much harder. This time it was anger and jealousy that deafened him to her voice. Desperate to get some rein on both, he forced himself to focus on the southernmost point of the beach, where the waves broke onto rocks. Three… Four… Five…

In real time he had no idea how long he stood counting wave after wave after wave, but he abandoned the task at number twenty-two. Whoever said the sea was calming was full of garbage!

*   *   *

She arrived home from the party at 2:41 a.m. Saturday. Brett knew the precise time because for the last hour and ten minutes he'd lain in bed watching his digital clock and thinking only of her. Prior to that, he'd spent the time since her departure watching the TV…and thinking only of her. His mind hadn't even had the room to accommodate images of the man she was with, despite the gut-eroding jealousy he felt towards him.

At 2:44 a.m., he heard the door of her bedroom open and close.

Then the only sound was the digits of the clock clicking over.

At 7:10 a.m., he heard her bedroom door open, then, a few seconds later, the brief, tell-tale creak of the bathroom door opening and closing.

Driven by desperation, he flung back the covers and bolted from his bed…

At 7:16 a.m., he was knocking urgently on the back door of his friend's house. Finally Jason answered it.

God knows where he'd have gone if no one had been home, but there was no way he could have stayed in the house with Jo there. He checked the water level in the kettle, switched on the power and opened the china cupboard. 'You want one, Jason?'

'In the middle of a fire? I don't think so. There *is* a fire, isn't there?' he asked. 'After all, what other reason could you have for waking me at this hour on a Saturday morning? *Uncaring that I may have someone here.*'

Only then did the extent of his presumptuousness dawn. 'Hell, mate, I'm sorry. I didn't think… You should've said something sooner.'

'Forgive me. These days it takes me at least a nano-second to make the transition from being blissfully asleep to being a victim of home invasion.'

'Look, I'm really sorry; consider me out of here.' He was already heading towards the door, but his friend shut it.

'Sit down, Brett,' he said. 'I'll get the coffee. Although I'm not sure it's going to do much good... If a dog looked like you do, I'd have it put down as an act of humanity.'

'Thanks, mate. Hold that thought and I'll try to muster up a bark.' His backside was halfway to a chair when he froze and glanced in the general direction of the bedrooms. 'Er...what about...?'

'Merely a hypothesis based on wishful thinking,' his friend said. 'Sit. I'll fix the coffee.'

A few minutes later a steaming mug of the beverage was set before him, along with a plate of cinnamon toast. Not feeling the least bit hungry, he shot a bemused frown at the man taking the chair opposite him. 'Er...did I say I wanted toast?'

Jason shook his head. 'No, the only thing you've uttered since sitting down is, "I'm going to have to kill her." But you look like you could use some food. Sleep doesn't look like it'd go astray either.'

'Blame my sister,' he muttered. 'She's the source of my problem.'

'So Meaghan's the one you want to kill?'

'Yeah, her too.' He picked up his cup, but then banged it back on the table. Too wired to stay seated, he prowled to the sink.

'Damn it, Jason, this whole situation is driving me nuts! I told myself I wasn't interested—at least I didn't *want* to be interested. I sure didn't need any more female emotional baggage in my life.

'And what happens?' he asked, pacing to the refrigerator. 'Whammo! I'm sideswiped by a raven-haired witch with the face of an angel and a body built for sin! None of which I'm supposed to notice, of course,' he said sardonically, pivoting, 'because not only is she barely out of high school, she's as trusting and naive as a kitten and still getting over some mongrel who saw her vulnerability and naivety as handy for some extra-marital recreation!

'So,' he continued, 'at the risk of suffering a hormone-induced nervous breakdown, I behave like the model gentleman from day one. I make sure I always wear a shirt, because the first time she saw me start to peel off my wet-suit I thought she was going to hyperventilate from shock. I'm careful to avoid any sexual innuendo, I try till I sweat blood not to notice when she parades around the house half naked, and when I can't take it any more I go and paddle out into a freezing winter Pacific, or—'

'Or come over here at all hours, make coffee, then sit around waiting for it to go cold so you can make another one,' Jason inserted.

'You're exaggerating.'

'Not by much. You've spent more time over here the last few weeks than you did in the whole time we were at school. And for God's sake, stop pacing!

'Look, Brett,' Jason continued, pouring himself another coffee. 'I don't have any idea of what sort of social life Joanna has, but I suspect I could go pretty close to calculating her diary based on the number of times you've "just dropped in" lately.' He grinned. 'Amazingly, though, on this occasion you haven't included her name in *every* sentence.'

Brett allowed himself a humourless laugh. 'I'd like to think that was a sign that I'm turning the corner and losing interest in her. Except the only things I'm losing are sanity and sleep.'

Sheer frustration had him emitting a growl and dragging his hand down his face. Hell, he hadn't even bothered to shave last night, or this morning! He'd religiously shaved twice a day from his university days, yet she'd managed to disrupt his life on such an elemental level that even his most ritualistic idiosyncrasies were being undermined by her.

Feeling almost utterly defeated, he slumped back into the chair. 'Jason...I *swear*, she's driving me out of my mind.'

'Why? Because she's not interested?'

Brett gave a harsh, ironic laugh. 'If only it were that

simple! If she'd stop sending out so many mixed messages and just post a *"thanks, but no thanks"* I'd get over it. I'm not a masochist. But it's like she's been testing me ever since she told me she trusted me—I mean she actually verbalised the phrase: "Now I know I can trust you."''

He shook his head. 'Being told by a drop-dead gorgeous woman that she trusts you… Well, now I know exactly how poor old Ken Evans felt in Year Eleven when that chick who was putting out for everybody else refused to go to the end of year dance with him because he was always so respectful of her she thought he deserved better!'

Jason laughed, whether at Ken's past or his present, Brett didn't know.

'What are these tests she's setting you?'

'Breathing, smiling, walking!' he said dryly. 'Oh, you know…it's kind of more the way she acts than anything else. If she was a few years older, and not so damnably innocent, I wouldn't doubt for a minute she was interested…' He paused and searched for words to explain.

'Well, it's not so much that she runs hot and cold. On some occasions I'll catch her sending me furtive looks, but the minute I make eye contact she gets this guilty blush…'

'Sure, because you caught her doing it and she's embarrassed.'

'Nah… It's more than that, Jason. She reacts as if…I don't know…like she's suddenly realised she's lusting after the devil himself. And let me tell you,' he added, 'when you know as much about her family's view of Old Nick as I do that can make you feel lower than a snake's belly.

'But then,' he continued, 'she's back to being her usual unselfconscious self—or at least she doesn't act self-conscious around *me*,' he qualified. 'In public she can glow neon if someone so much as asks her if she wants salt on her chips, but with good old Brett she's so at ease she thinks nothing of parading around in sexy little negligées. Or—*get this, mate*—knocking on my bedroom door late at night wrapped only in a hand towel to ask sleep-destroying questions such as can she borrow one of my razors to shave her legs.'

That particular incident had happened last week, but coming after the incident with the dress and her non-stop chatter about Steve it had made him more angry than aroused. At least that was what he'd told himself through the ensuing sleepless night at any rate.

Brett went on to recount the incidents of the dress and the massage to Jason, who, of course, by now found the whole thing totally amusing. *He would; his dates all wore shirts.*

'Give me a break, here, Jason... She's driving me nuts! I mean, take the massage scenario...it's the oldest trick in the book for both sexes, right?'

'Mmm. Classic preliminary lead-in to a seduction,' his friend agreed.

'Exactly! Except Jo acts like she *knows* I'm not going to make a move. There she was, lying under my hands purring like a well-satisfied cat, and expecting me to act like a damned eunuch! I know she's naive and— *What's so funny?*' he demanded of his suddenly chuckling friend.

Jason merely shook his head. 'Er...tell me, Brett,' he said, trying to contain his mirth. 'How has she reacted when you've tried to put the moves on her?'

'What moves?' he snarled. 'I told you; I've nearly killed myself trying to keep my hands off her. The closest I've come to losing it was yesterday. I was a heartbeat away from kissing her—and, damn it, Jason, I *know* she wanted me to!' Recalling the moment, he raked his hand through his hair. 'I could *feel* it, you know. I couldn't have stopped if I wanted to,' he admitted. 'Then suddenly she bolts, like I'm the plague or something, and starts rabbiting on like a narrator on a TV doco. I tell you, mate, she—'

He broke off as Jason, quaking with mirth, staggered out of his chair holding his stomach.

'Oh, God...' his friend cackled, his eyes tearing. 'This is priceless... I think I'm going to wet myself.'

'I'm glad the sorry state of my life is such a source of amusement to you...*mate!*'

'I...I'm sorry,' Jason managed, wiping his eyes. 'But I've just put two and two together and I think I know what your problem is. It's just all suddenly added up.'

'Well, maths never was my strong point,' Brett said testily, irritated at being the source of his friend's amusement and in the dark as to why. 'So why don't you just give me the answer, Einstein.'

Jason's grin was as wide as Sydney Heads. *'Joanna thinks you're gay.'*

CHAPTER THIRTEEN

'*GAY*! You think I'm *gay*?'

Brett got his answer when she had to grab the bookcase to keep from collapsing with shock! That she was so obviously dumbfounded sent his ego nose-diving even further; his anger, however, was probably burning holes in what was left of the ozone layer.

'Y-you mean you *aren't*?'

'No, damn it, I'm not!'

Her eyes were wide as saucers, her mouth gaping, and she was taking two steps backwards for every advancing one of his.

'Now would you mind telling me why you'd jump to such a crazy conclusion?' Hell, here he'd been turning hormonal cartwheels every time he so much as looked at her, while he'd made all the sexual impact of a slice of bread on her!

'Well?' he demanded, when she merely continued to stammer and stare at him as if he'd suddenly grown a second head.

'I... Th... *Oomph*!' The bookcase brought her stammering back-pedalling to an abrupt end. On her right she was hemmed in by a turn-of-the-century wing-backed chair. Brett braced his arm against the wall to her left to close off that escape route.

'Well, Jo? I'm dying to hear how you came to make this insane assessment of my sexuality.'

'Um...well, for lots of reasons, really,' she said.

'*Lots of reasons?* Gee, when you set out to mutilate a guy's ego, you don't pull your punches, do you?' he said. 'I take it one of these reasons is my friendship with Jason?'

'P-partly.'

'I hate to tell you this, Jo, but your small-town homophobic attitude is—'

'I am *not* homophobic!' Her denial was loud and emphatic. 'If I was I wouldn't have stayed here with you when I'd been led to believe you were—'

'I know what you believed, Jo!' he cut in, not needing to be hit over the head with the fact yet again. 'What, besides me having a gay friend, gave you this wacky idea?'

'Lots of things.'

'Will you *stop* saying that! *What* things?'

She sighed under the weight of his glare. 'Well…first, just after you moved in, I told Karessa I wasn't comfortable living with a man I knew nothing about. And she said I didn't have to worry about you…' she swallowed nervously '…because you weren't interested in women—'

'*Temporarily!*' he jumped in. 'I wasn't interested *temporarily!*'

'Well, *she* didn't say that. The reason she gave me was because you were still getting over Toni.'

Brett groaned. 'And you naturally assumed Toni was short for Anthony rather than Antonia.'

'I didn't know Toni could be a girl's name. And you didn't do anything to correct my impression!' The uncharacteristic tartness of her tone dumbfounded him almost as much as her accusation.

'*Excuse me?*'

'Well, you didn't,' she said. 'You don't act like normal straight men.'

'And this observation of yours is based on what? Your vast experience with men?'

Her only response was a blush of discomfiture that he refused to feel guilty about; after all *he* was the victim in this. She, on the other hand, had jumped to conclusions on the *flimsiest* of circumstantial evidence.

'Look, Brett,' she said, clearly flustered. 'I just meant you seemed different to—'

'All those *other* men in your jet-setting past?'

Her hands went onto her hips, and for the first time since he'd met her Joanna didn't look anything like the calm, serene person by whom he'd become so fascinated. But her sexiness sure hadn't diminished with this sudden leap in attitude.

'I may not,' she said, 'be as sophisticated as most women my age, but a person doesn't need to have ridden a horse to recognise one.'

Hearing her make a statement with such an overt sexual connotation sent his jaw slack even as it curled nerve-endings in other parts of his anatomy. But, in the absence of an ensuing sultry smile or lewd look, he belatedly realised Jo hadn't intended any *double entendre*.

'And whether you like it or not,' she continued, 'your behaviour *isn't* what I've come to expect from most men. Until I met you, Steve was the only man I'd known who hadn't treated me like a servant or been nice to me because he wanted to sleep with me.

'And *so*,' she went on, 'because you *were* a gentleman—didn't paw me or want to get me into bed—'

Wanna bet?

'Plus you displayed other signs that tended to suggest a—'

'I *what*?' he exploded, vowing that if he turned out impotent as a result of this, he'd sue her to hell and back!

'Oh, for heaven's sake, Brett! I don't mean you come across as effeminate!' she snapped, reading his mind. 'But let's face it, you cook better than most women, you can recognise who designed a dress just by looking at it—'

'Says who?'

'*I've seen you do it,*' she told him. 'At the fund-raiser you could tell who designed my dress—'

'Only because I saw the label when I was buttoning you into the damned thing!'

'Oh…'

'Yes, *oh*.'

'Well, you can't deny you know more than most men about feminine things like clothes and…and style and co-ordinating colours and stuff.'

'It'd be hard not to!' he snapped. 'My mother's a professional decorator and Dad was a fashion guru!'

He grunted, staggering slightly, as she shoved him hard in the chest and having caught him off-guard, ducked under his arm.

'Look, I'm sorry; all right? But you have to understand that on top of all those things, and after reading that article—'

'It's *in print* that I'm gay?'

'Oh, no! It's just a general article on how…er…how to tell if a guy is gay. I di—'

'*Get it.*'

'Huh?'

'Get…me…the…article.'

As she darted from the room with the speed of the very desperate, he slumped onto the sofa and dropped his head in his hands. There was no longer any doubt in his mind that God was definitely female; a male wouldn't do this to one of his own.

'I won't be long!' he heard her yell. 'I've just got to try and remember what magazine it's in.'

He didn't bother responding. She had to have eighty assorted magazines and journals which she kept in a cane trunk in her room. Perhaps by the time she found it he'd have managed to make sense out of the whole bizarre situation. For he couldn't deny he'd been thrown for a loop. Big time.

Discovering the woman he was attracted to had perceived him to be homosexual could really spin a guy out. It was worse than being rejected because it meant he hadn't even made enough sensual impact to warrant *being* rejected. It was as if he and his sexuality were so inconsequential that they were invisible to her on all levels and discovering he was heterosexual would count for nought.

But, damn it! He *couldn't* believe that he could feel the way he did about Jo without her sensing at least some level of awareness. Hell, if that was case he was in danger of falling for a brick wall or a bird bath!

Brett's head came up at the sound of the doorbell to find Jo watching him from the entrance of the room, a magazine in her hand.

'Er…that'll be Steve,' she said.

Great, just what he needed to be confronted with right now—her damn boyfriend! 'And where are we off to today?' he asked snidely. 'Another candy-floss-eating excursion?'

Her mouth tightened. 'We were just going to have lunch here.'

The bell acted as a bleep for the four-letter expletive he muttered. Not trusting himself to speak, he got to his feet, crossed the room and took the magazine from her clenched hand.

'Brett, wait! I…I really am sorry. I… I…' She shrugged. 'I don't know what else to say.'

'Then quit while you're ahead,' he said, striding from the room towards the bedrooms.

The magazine was the typical glossy affair women favoured. It was titled *Nineties You* and, according to the lightning blot cutting diagonally across it, this was the launch edition. He flopped back on the bed and thumbed his way to page nine.

'IS IT WORTH THE EFFORT?' was the main title, then, in smaller, vivid red letters: *'How To Tell If The Hunk You've Been Eyeing At The Bar Is Interested In You Or Your Brother Before You Put In The Hard Work.'*

The first paragraph was a diatribe about how women today faced two major problems when it came to men, those being that all the nicest ones were taken and all the best-looking ones were gay. The writer then said that there were signs to assist females on the make from wasting valuable time batting their eyelashes at guys who were going to be 'non-starters' in the passion stakes.

Brett tried to imagine Joanna in a predatory role, batting her thick black lashes. He forced himself to banish the thought when his body started taking an interest in what he'd intended to be purely intellectual speculation. Directing his attention back to the magazine, he continued reading, skimming the page until he reached the magazine's warning that women should be suspicious of 'any gorgeous-looking male who seems to know more about decorating than you do and whose advice on your wardrobe actually makes sense!'

Undoubtedly Jason would get a chuckle out of that, but the damning statement hadn't done *his* cause any good; there was no mention of giving the benefit of the doubt to guys who through no fault of their own were genetically predisposed to good taste. Which meant that yesterday when he'd been giving Jo advice on how to dress he'd only been pulling the noose tighter around his neck!

He tossed the magazine onto the floor amid a chorus of expletives. Then, realising he was overreacting he tried to get a rein on his irritation. Fair enough, Jo had been way off beam with her assumptions, but *why* was he feeling so angry about what should have been a funny situation?

Because, his ego answered, *you feel Jo should've been so overpowered by your machismo that she'd forget ever reading all this garbage.*

He drew a long breath and forced himself to try and see things from where she'd been standing. Being objective, he supposed that someone as unworldly as Jo could have misinterpreted things. Especially since he'd nearly killed himself trying to keep his distance. The truism about the road to hell being paved with good intentions had certainly been proven out in this instance.

The problem was he still wanted her in the worst way. But even now, knowing the truth, Jo would subconsciously have a hard time getting past the notion of what she'd perceived him to be. And then, of course, there was good old Steve...

'G'day, mate. How're things?'

'Fine thanks, Brett.' Cooper smiled. 'Yourself?'

'Fighting fit. Joanna, can I have a word with you for a moment?'

His easy request had her looking nervous and suspicious as she rose from the attractively laid table over which she and Steve were sharing a frozen cannelloni. Brett knew it was frozen because, while Jo was competent in the kitchen, her imagination pretty much ended at steak, lamb chops and three vegetables.

Excusing herself, she followed Brett through the kitchen to the laundry. It was obvious she was both curious and anxious about what he wanted to say.

Fiddling with her hair in a pseudo-casual manner that didn't quite work with the way she was gnawing her lip, she waited for him to speak.

Brett deliberately kept her waiting.

'Well?' she prompted, shifting her feet restlessly.

'I read the article.'

'And?'

'And it's the greatest load of crap I've ever seen put into print,' he said calmly. 'I suggest that if you don't want to make a goose of yourself in future you disregard every bit of it.'

Colour flooded her face. She gave a curt nod and turned to leave, but before she could take a step Brett hauled her into his arms and backed her against the wall.

The kiss was intended to teach her a lesson about jumping to conclusions. It was going to be the hardest, hottest kiss of her young life. But the plan he'd so coolly calculated while showering went down the drain the moment he felt the fragile curves of her body against his. Immediately he lessened the force of his lips on her oh, so soft moist ones and offered an oral apology by soothingly stroking his tongue across her lower lip from one corner to the other. But a rush of desire cut short his patience and, desperate to savour more of her sweetness, he tried to coax her mouth open. He was so convinced he could wear her down, so caught up in the need to do so, that it was several seconds before it registered she was struggling against him.

He pulled back instantly to find her face furious. 'You don't have to grope me to prove a point,' she said, her voice tight.

Before Brett could deny the accusation, which in part would've been a lie anyway, she was already rushing back to Cooper. Once again he'd managed to come off feeling like the world's biggest jerk.

CHAPTER FOURTEEN

CORRECTING Joanna's misconceptions regarding his sexuality didn't work in Brett's favour.

Where once she'd seemed relatively at ease in his presence, now her behaviour was reserved and circumspect. No more did she settle on the sofa dressed for bed and reading snippets from magazines. Gone were her spontaneous smiles and excited revelations of things she'd done, was planning to do or found interesting.

Brett might have taken some consolation from the fact Steve Cooper had ceased to be so prominent a feature in her life if her social calendar hadn't become a production line of Kyles, Adams and Camerons. These days her presence in the house seemed to be limited to merely sleeping and personal hygiene. They'd not shared a meal together since he'd kissed her twelve days ago, and on the rare occasions it looked as if they might be in the house together for long enough to have a conversation her contribution to it was usually, 'Oh, hello; I'm going out now.' Whereafter she either retreated to her room or went for long walks on the beach.

Brett told himself this didn't bother him. He'd had the week from hell and more than enough to occupy his time and mind without wondering about what Jo was doing in her life. Today had been wall-to-wall meetings at the agency, fine-tuning detail on the possible London purchase prior to Meaghan flying out to the UK on Saturday. Then his lawyer had phoned with the news that the couple selling the property he wanted had decided to divorce and the 'injured party' was now pettily refusing to sell; negotiations had come to a grinding halt. And, as if that wasn't enough, yesterday, when he'd been all set to sign an eighteen-month deal with a network to produce a lifestyle programme which would feature everything from DIY home improvements to health and fitness and financial management, he'd discovered that the network manager wanted control of which presenters were hired to handle each segment. Having been down that disastrous road once before, Brett was holding firm that he was the one with the final yea or nay in that area.

No, he decided, entering the semi-darkened house after yet another business dinner with the network's owner, which had resolved nothing, the last thing he needed was a perky, scantily clad Jo keeping his hormones on edge.

For a moment he considered going straight to bed, then opted to grab a beer and try and unwind a bit in front of the late-night sports show. It wasn't until nearly an hour later, when he went to the laundry door to check it was locked, that he saw the huddled figure sitting on the back patch of lawn.

'Joanna, is that you?'

She'd been sitting so perfectly still that it wasn't until she reacted to the sound of his voice that the external sensor light went on. Clad in an anorak and jeans, she sat on the ground hugging her knees while a better than light offshore breeze lifted her hair back from her face.

'You know you can set this light to stay on,' he said, doing so as he spoke. 'You're lucky you weren't locked out,' he chided, more roughly than he'd intended.

He thought her shoulders shrugged, but then again it could have been a shiver. Her head was already turning back towards the beach when she said, 'It wouldn't be the first time. Don't worry, I'll lock up when I come in.'

It was clearly a dismissal, but Brett ignored it. 'Why on earth are you sitting out here in the dark?' He was already out of the door and negotiating the steps from the house to the tiered yard as he spoke.

'Thinking.' The one-word response was flat and lifeless. But also, he realised, tinged with hurt.

Ignoring the cold, he planted himself on the patch of ground next to her. She offered no sound of protest, nor even looked at him. Resting his elbows on his knees, he joined in her silent scrutiny of the horizon, content to simply sit with her. Which he supposed either made him easily pleased or certifiable for risking exposure for a woman who was not only rugged up against the cold but seemingly intent on freezing him out as well.

After about five minutes he decided it was the latter, and, disgusted with the pathos of his desperation, he shifted his weight to get to his feet.

'I really thought she'd forgive me...'

Instantly the sad, soft voice changed his mind about leaving.

'I thought,' she continued, 'that once she had time to...to calm down, she'd realise I wasn't so much rejecting her beliefs as following my own.'

'You're talking about your sister...' He spoke hesitantly, not from uncertainty but for fear he'd say something which would prompt her to clam up again.

'She hates me, Brett,' she whispered unsteadily.

The desolation behind her tearful words wrung his heart.

'She really, really hates me. We're the only family either of us has left an—and she...she wants nothing to do w-with m-m—' Her voice broke on a half-sob.

Brett wasn't sure whether he'd pulled her to his chest in a bid to comfort her or if she'd flung herself there, but as his arms closed around her clothes-bulky figure he prayed for the ability to be able to absorb every bit of her pain.

'I've tried to explain to her.' Tears and his shoulder muffled her words. 'I've written to her every day, even though she...she wouldn't answer... And today...today, was her birthday, so I...I rang her. To...to say happy birthday and...and...'

'Shh, honey,' Brett soothed, gently stroking the back of her head. 'Take it easy... It's going to be all right.'

Her head shook against his chest. 'Th-that's what I kept t-telling myself. That it would...work out. But it's n-not... F-Faith's never going to forgive me...I know that now.'

Her long, shuddering sigh was so sadly resigned that he wished he held the power to right this wrong in her world. He didn't know all the ins and outs of her falling out with her sister, but he knew the older woman had abandoned Joanna at a time when she was vulnerable. The trouble was, he sensed Joanna's trusting heart would always be vulnerable, whether she was twenty-two or ninety-two.

Even now, as she cuddled against him, one arm around his back and the other clutching his jumper, Brett knew she was seeking and expecting nothing more than comfort. So, with Herculean effort, he steeled himself against the tempting self-delusion that he would be acting with only the noblest of intentions were he to tumble her back onto the grass and kiss away her pain until she experienced only the most exquisite pleasure. She'd confided in him because she trusted him. And because she did he couldn't abuse that trust by lying even to himself.

For an indeterminable length of time, that was both painfully long and conversely not long enough, he simply held her, making soothing, murmuring noises and words which made no sense and required no response. They were the same generic phrases he'd used all those years ago to comfort Meaghan, but then as now, they did little to ease his own pain of the moment. Most guys he knew complained that crying women freaked them, but they straight out broke Brett's heart. None more so than Jo.

As the tears lessened and her sobs faded to hiccups she started to speak again. In an act of non-verbal encouragement and support he tucked her tighter against him.

'I always imagined that Faith was just like me. That if Mother and Father hadn't been around we'd have been able to laugh and be like real sisters. Do things like normal families did—go to the movies or…or away on vacations together. But it didn't happen. Nothing changed. Except Faith took over the role of disciplining me. Telling me what to do, what to think…

'I knew then I had to make a stand if I ever wanted to have a chance at a normal life, of being like other girls my age and having nice clothes and a boyfriend… I thought that was the easiest place to start—with a boyfriend. So during the Christmas vacation, when a boy in my class started paying attention to me when he came into the store, I didn't ignore him, like I was supposed to do with boys…' She paused and drew a long breath before continuing.

'He started coming every day when I was taking my lunchbreak out behind the store shed. One day when he tried to kiss me I let him. No one had ever kissed me before, not even my parents.'

The concept so flabbergasted Brett that he couldn't express his disbelief. What kind of parents didn't kiss their child? The idea was incomprehensible to him.

'It was a really innocent kiss,' Jo went on, 'but the next thing I knew Faith was there screaming about how she'd set the police on him if he ever came near me again and physically dragging me back into the store. For three days she only spoke to me to quote Scripture and lecture me about sins of the flesh.' She sighed. 'Then she took me to Brisbane and enrolled me in boarding school.'

Brett refrained from saying that was the best thing that could have happened to her. When a boarding school represented freedom, it gave a whole new meaning to grim.

'When I finished school and went back home to work in the store, I knew with absolute certainty that I couldn't live my life like her. I didn't know *exactly* what I wanted to do as a career, just that I needed to get away and be a part of the world I'd read about and experienced little bits of when I was away at school.

'I tried to explain to her how I felt, but she wouldn't listen. She kept telling me that vanity and self-absorption were sinful, and that my obligations to God and my family were at the store. I decided that as soon as I could save enough money I'd leave... And then I met Andrew.'

She paused, her body moving gently against his in re-action to a long, soulful sigh.

'He was a sales representative for a tractor company and had a flat he stayed in when he was in the region. I know he took me for a fool, but I truly had no idea he was mar-ried. None. Until his wife and son turned up on the doorstep three months later while he was out of town.'

Anger flared in every muscle of Brett's body. The word *'Bastard'* which hissed though his clenched teeth was too complimentary to the mongrel.

'I'm not sure if I was more heartbroken or humiliated, but I went home believing Faith would stick by me.' Her laugh was brittle and without humour. 'I guess that made me a fool twice over.'

'It's not foolish to hope that the people you love will love you back,' Brett told her, aching from the extent of the hurt inflicted on her young life.

'It feels foolish,' she said bleakly. 'But I'm not going to be foolish any more. I don't think it's wrong to want to be happy. To try and find fulfilment and contentment in life if it doesn't hurt others. It's *my* life and I want to experience it, not just wait quietly for it to end.

'Maybe I *am* selfish and self-obsessed, Brett,' she said quietly. 'But I just can't feel guilty about wanting to pursue my dreams.'

'Oh, Joanna,' he said softly. 'You don't have to feel guilty... If ever anyone has earned the right to happiness it's you.'

As he spoke he stroked her hair, becoming so mesmer-ised by its cool silkiness that he kept combing his fingers through it over and over, until the action matched the rhythm of the sea. The silky tresses slipped from his fingers each time a wave lapped the shore. He didn't look at her, but kept staring out at the night-darkened sea, as if he could somehow prolong the moment when this would end and she'd move away.

All too soon she began to shift restlessly, but in an act of defiance his fingers continued their rhythm.

'Brett...'

'Mmm?'

'Will you kiss me?'

So this was what cardiac arrest felt like!

Now he was looking at her! 'K-kiss you?'

She nodded as calmly as if she'd requested a cup of tea and he'd asked if she wanted milk.

'Why?' he heard himself ask, and started questioning both their sanity.

'Because the other day you were angry with me. And you made me angry.' Turquoise eyes locked on his. 'But I've kept wondering what it would be like if we weren't angry.'

Brett heaved in a long, controlling breath and held it. He had to because he was going to drown in those eyes. 'It would be,' he said, his hand closing on her chin, 'a lot more than you've bargained for, Joanna. It would be hot...passionate...and very hard to stop.'

'I see...' Her gaze lowered to his neck. 'I've been imagining it'd be soft...gentle...' He felt her inhale before lifting her eyes back to his. *'And very hard to stop.'*

In that nano-second of time, even before his mouth touched hers, Brett knew he was in love. With her. With everything about her. Her simplistic honesty, her beauty, her naivety; *everything*.

He had expected to have to hold himself in check, but it wasn't necessary. The tenderness he felt for this woman gave him a patience he'd not credited himself with; it was no sacrifice to gently brush his lips with feather-lightness over hers instead of ravishing them. Nor was it a hardship for the tip of his tongue to trace their shape in slow, sensual exploration rather than plunge into their depths as he'd fantasised. And the glorious reward for his patience was the feel of her arm snaking around his neck and her fingers spreading against the base of his skull. There was further reward when her mouth parted to invite him deeper, and in the whispery groan she made when he declined, to tug lightly on her lower lip instead.

Then all Brett could do was lean back and let their combined weight flatten him against the ground as he lost himself in what he knew was truly the first kiss of his life. Even in the plethora of emotions which poured through him when her own tongue took the trembling initiative to seek what it wanted, tenderness was still the most prominent.

How much time passed between then and when he threaded his fingers through Jo's hair and was jarred by the variation in texture, he didn't know, but it was only then he became aware of the soft misty rain falling. Had it been summer, he wouldn't have found it intrusive enough to curb his pleasure, but the chill winter air demanded common sense.

Reluctantly he eased his mouth from hers, finding some measure of compensation for the loss in her slowly opening eyes. Once again they were teal, not turquoise, but this time they were sensuously drowsy as they surveyed him. That she still hadn't noticed the rain, now falling quite heavily, was both flattering and amusing.

Smiling, he drew a finger down her elegant nose. 'It's raining.'

'That's okay; my coat's waterproof.'

He laughed at her vague, automatic response. 'Unfortunately I'm not,' he said, encouraging her onto her side.

After quickly getting to his feet he helped her up, then, holding her hand, started to hurry towards the house. His mind was still a jumble as to what he was going to do when he got there.

'Brett…' she said, stopping suddenly and making him turn to her. 'I like it better when we're not angry.'

Her simple, uncomplicated honesty created a warmth within him that negated the now teeming rain and a sweater too wet to offer protection against the wind. If he were to be equally as truthful with her, he'd tell her he'd fallen in love with her.

But he wouldn't.

He couldn't.

Because he'd fallen in love with a woman who hadn't experienced enough of life to be bound by his expectations of it.

He didn't know what he was going to do about his predicament, and the wisest, safest thing was to suspend things until he did.

In that instant he felt a momentary flash of anger towards her for inspiring a tenderness capable of overpowering his desire for her, a love that demanded he consider her needs ahead of his own for fear of hurting her. Never had he felt so tormented or uncertain of himself. And in the utter confusion that reigned between his head, heart and hormones, he clutched desperately at humour to get him through.

'Joanna...' he said, sending a pointed look to the raining skies. 'Exactly how long can you tread water?'

CHAPTER FIFTEEN

THE water was cold and grey as dawn lit the morning, and chopped up by a wind that couldn't make up its mind from which direction to blow. Even in a wetsuit Brett couldn't last more than fifteen minutes in it. After a night spent staring at the ceiling, he'd figured a good solid workout against the elements might go some way to clearing his confused mind and emotions. In theory the idea had seemed good; in reality it had just left him colder and more agitated.

The glow of the bathroom light up at the house told him Jo was now up and about; the instinctive part of him wanted to bound up the steps and take up where the rain had interrupted them last night, but logic told him following his instincts was the worst thing he could do. As they'd done all night, brain and hormones continued to debate the issue as he crossed the sand and climbed the steps to the house. When there was still no clear victor by the time he reached the patio, he decided he needed an impartial adjudicator.

Trying to get his circulation going again, Brett jogged the three houses to Jason's place. His friend being a builder, who was invariably on site at seven to issue his crews with their daily work schedules, Brett figured he would be halfway through his breakfast by now.

Jason answered the door on the first knock with a steaming cup in his hand and curiously raised eyebrows. 'Let me guess,' he said, stepping aside to motion Brett inside. 'You've locked yourself out and didn't want to wake Joanna, huh?'

Brett raked his still dripping hair. 'She's already awake.'

'Then why are you here, dressed for the invasion of the frogmen?'

'Because she's awake. The surf sucks. I haven't slept. And God's female.'

'Rrrr-ight.' Jason nodded. 'And exactly how big was the wave that caused your concussion?'

'About five-foot-three… I'm in love with her, mate.'

'Gosh, there's a surprise.' The droll response was accompanied by a wry grin. 'I could've told you that weeks ago. Does she know?'

'Hell, no! That's why I'm here.'

Red eyebrows rose. 'You want *me* to tell her?'

'No!' Brett snapped, aghast. 'I've decided I don't want her to know.'

'Can I ask *why*?'

'Because if she felt the same way it would ruin her life.'

Jason chuckled. 'I wouldn't say you're *that* hard to put up with, mate.'

Brett let the joke roll past him. 'The truth is she's too young for me. And I don't just mean in years. We're at totally opposite poles of our life. She's chomping at the bit to experience all the excitement and bright lights of the world, and I'm…well, I'm ready for all the dull, boring stuff like marriage and kids and…and retirement.'

'Retirement!' Jason roared with laughter. 'You're not even thirty-five yet, mate!'

'Damn it, Jason! You know what I mean!' Frustration was eating Brett alive. 'Jo's had a rotten life to date. She's never had a chance to be anything but what other people wanted her to be. I love her too much to want to be responsible for robbing her of even one of her dreams or ambitions.'

'And you know for a fact that love, marriage and kids aren't included in those dreams and ambitions, do you?'

Brett blinked. 'Well, no. That is, I don't *know* that. Actually…given Jo's obsession with family, even one that's treated her like dirt, I'd have to say marriage and kids *would* be on her agenda,' he mused.

'Then what's the problem? Why not tell her how you feel?'

'*Because*, Jason,' he said testily, wondering if his friend was being deliberately obtuse, 'she's not ready for that sort of commitment *now*. And I'm not going to put her in a position where she gets confused and thinks she is.'

'God, you're an arrogant so and so, Brett! Don't you think Jo ought to have some input as to what she is and isn't ready for? For that matter, has it occurred to you that she might *not* be as bowled over by a declaration of love from you for her to even contemplate changing her life on your behalf?'

'Of course it has! Hell, that's another reason I'm not going to say anything to her. The mere thought of having her toss my feelings back in my face is excruciating. What's more, she'd probably feel guilty about it.'

For several moments the other man just stared at him, then he ruefully shook his head. 'So, if you're not going to tell her how you feel, what are you planning to do? Wallow in the misery of unrequited love without even bothering to find out if it's necessary?'

'I don't know! I thought I had problems when I just wanted to sleep with her…but *this*! Hell, Jason, by loving her it's not like I'm just asking her for her body; I'm asking her for her heart, her dreams and her whole life.'

His friend's face was an incomprehensible blank.

Brett dragged a resigned hand over his face. 'I guess the only thing I can do is simply get over her.'

'You're going to "simply get over her",' Jason echoed, then shook his head. 'Listen, mate, go take a shower before circulation to your brain freezes entirely. Meanwhile, in the hope of sparing at least one of us more of your rabid self-delusions and rambling, I'm going to work. Lock up when you leave.'

Brett waited until thirty minutes past the time Jo always left for work before deciding it was safe to go home. While he knew avoiding her *every* morning wasn't going to be possible, at least it granted him some more time to come to terms with the decision he'd made before he had to face her.

'*Why not tell her how you feel?*' Ha! As a sounding-board, Jason made a good vacuum. Still, with a shower and several cups of coffee under his belt, Brett felt sufficiently sure of the decision he'd made to offer a cheeky wink in response to an elderly neighbour's surprised and speculative expression at the sight of him crossing the street in a sweatsuit the size of which clearly identified it as Jason's.

But while the curiosity of a nosy neighbour didn't surprise him, the feminine giggle that greeted him a moment after he'd entered the house did. His heart flipped over at the sight of Jo's radiant amusement, before he reminded himself that he *wasn't* pleased to see her.

'And you've been giving *me* wardrobe advice?' she teased, a hand on her hip accentuating the way the black angora dress held her curves.

'What are you doing here? Why aren't you at work?' He sounded alarmed only because that was exactly what he was: alarmed that the emotions this woman stirred with her curvaceous figure and beautiful face weren't being influenced by his noble decision not to act on his feelings for her.

'Meaghan rang while you were out surfing,' she said, advancing towards him on long shapely legs. 'Apparently some hitch has occurred with her passport and she needs you at the office to handle last-minute stuff with lawyers while she sorts it out. She sounded really frazzled and upset and said I was to personally give you the message, then catch a ride in with you ASAP.'

Oh, wonderful. Cooped up in a car with her, her exotic perfume and a dress that was going to show even more thigh when she sat down. Oh, yeah, just what he needed!

'When did you get this?' she asked, climbing into the black Saab after he'd reversed it out of the garage. Yep, he'd been right! The damn dress did creep beyond the heights of a man's sanity when she sat down.

'A week ago. Day before I put Mum's in to be repaired.'

'Oh.' She gave a sheepish smile. 'Guess that proves we haven't exactly seen much of one another lately.'

'I've been busy.'

There was a long moment of silence before she said, 'And, um…what's been keeping you so busy?'

Riding shotgun on my libido around you! he thought, forcing himself to shrug. 'This and that. Business, plans for the new house. It's not easy moving your life from one country to another.'

'I see. And, um…are you doing anything tonight?'

'Why?'

Her cheeks pinkened beneath her make-up. 'Well, we— that is, the staff at the agency—have organised a surprise dinner for Meaghan tonight. I thought that you might like to come.'

Brett gripped the steering wheel so hard he marvelled that it didn't crush. If ever there was a case of having to decide whether to answer the door to opportunity at the risk of getting your fingers jammed in the hinge, this was it.

'I know Meaghan would love it if you came,' she said, filling a silence in which the tension was almost tangible. 'And, um…I've already said I'll be bringing a guest. But since I didn't get around to asking anyone yet…it's going to mess up the numbers. You'd really be helping me out.'

And helping himself into an insane asylum! God, it was hard enough to keep his hands off her in broad daylight when they were sitting in bumper-to-bumper traffic; he'd never manage it at the end of a night spent listening to her chatter and laugh—

'I can't do it!' he blurted aloud.

For a moment she looked so disappointed Brett was a heartbeat from changing his mind, then she laughed. A very wry laugh. 'I suppose you've got a hot date, huh?'

'As a matter of fact I *do*.' Brett told himself it wasn't so much a lie as his sub-conscious pushing him into activating his decision to get over her.

'Oh… Well, that's all right,' she said airily. 'I'm sure I'll find somebody to make up the numbers.'

Brett was sure she would too. It wasn't as if she didn't have a cast of thousands phoning her day and night!

For the remainder of the trip they both contributed to a rigid silence, during which time Brett vowed that once he got back from dealing with whatever disaster awaited him at the agency, the first thing he was going to do was dig out his old address book!

It was a minor boost to his ego that the first woman he phoned was almost beside herself with distress at not being able to accept his invitation. 'Oh, Brett…I wish I could! Gosh, you should've called me sooner. I've already made arrangements to go to a business function with my husband. But, hey, he's flying interstate on business for two weeks tomorrow, so how about tomorrow night?'

Brett decided he'd scored a moral and possibly limb-saving victory in declining the offer, even *before* he learned that her recently acquired husband owned a martial arts school.

The second candidate on his list was both surprised and pleased to hear from him. Naturally she displayed the right amount of irritation at being called at only six hours' notice for a Friday night date, but Brett knew this was just one of those things women did. Rather than being irritated by it, he told himself he was relieved to be back dealing with a woman who knew how to 'play the game'.

By the time Jo arrived home he had everything under control, at least as far as organisation went. But he couldn't say that her cheerful revelation about having found a date for the evening didn't gnaw at his guts.

'You might know him,' she said. 'Grant Farr… He's a model from the agency, and very fond of Meaghan, so he was thrilled to be asked.'

Brett didn't know him. Didn't want to know him. And he would bet both his lungs that the jerk hadn't agreed to go with Joanna because of his supposed fondness for Meaghan! He made damn sure he was gone from the house before the guy arrived!

Suzanne Wells was tall, auburn-haired and ten years older than Jo.

The daughter of two prominent actors, her upbringing had been as liberal as Brett's, although, unlike him, she'd been educated to within an inch of her life; she held PhDs in History and English Literature, and a degree in Political Science. Currently she was compiling research on the development of the theatre in the South Pacific while trying to increase her flying hours so she could get a commercial pilot's licence.

A charming, witty and entertaining dinner companion, Suzanne wasn't the least bit hesitant in letting Brett know that she was recently divorced and not averse to some horizontal recreation on a purely casual basis. Brett accepted her invitation for coffee, convinced her terms suited him right down to the ground.

Unfortunately that was all that suited him.

The reality was he got more excited shaving than he did kissing Suzanne, and despite his best efforts to rally his enthusiasm, her practised seduction techniques lacked the impact of the dinner bill on his credit card. Within twenty-five minutes of entering her apartment Brett had exited it and was on his way home, making mental bets with himself as to whether or not Jo would be there.

She wasn't. She came in four hours and seven minutes later at 4:04 a.m. A fact that didn't, however, prevent her from being disgustingly bright-eyed and bushy-tailed when Brett discovered her dressed and reading a magazine as she ate breakfast at eight the next morning.

'Hi!' she said. 'How did your date go?'

The effort it took to produce a smile and a response that

wasn't a lie was painful. 'I'm not going to complain. Er...how was your night?'

'Great! We had so much fun!' She grinned. 'Your sister might be a little the worse for wear, though.'

'I'll let you know when I get back from the airport,' he grumbled, dissatisfied with her answer.

'Oh, I won't be here,' she said airily. 'I'm going out in about an hour.'

'Geez, considering the time you got in, there really wasn't any point in Grant going home, was there?' he asked snidely.

She took instant offence. 'For your information I'm not going out with Grant! And if I was ever going to invite someone to stay the night I'd be polite enough to consult you in advance.'

'Don't bother! Because the answer would be *no*! And who the hell are you going out with anyway?' he demanded.

'*None*,' she said, jumping to her feet, 'of your business, you...you...*idiot*!' And with that she snatched up the magazine and stormed out of the back door.

By the time Brett had recovered from her unprecedented display of temper, and the fact he'd just made one hell of a fool of himself, Jo was a distant figure heading south along the beach. The impulse to go after her and apologise warred with the desire to go after her and kiss her senseless.

In the end it was a phone call from his excited niece, demanding to know how long he was going to be, that solved his dilemma.

When he next saw Jo, on Sunday morning, she was her usual grudge-free self. Not surprisingly she was going out. *Again.* But this time Brett didn't ask where or with whom, nor reveal the sense of abject despair he'd felt when Meaghan had mentioned Jo's name amongst the list of agency staff who'd expressed interest in spending time at the London agency should the purchase go through.

For any twenty-two-year-old the chance of having their

airfare paid and the guarantee of employment in one of the world's most famous cities would be an exciting opportunity. But Brett knew that for Jo it would mean far more than that; for Jo it would represent the attainment of one of her wildest and most cherished dreams.

Which was why he'd told his sister that, though he wanted no further part in the running of the agency, if she did end up opening a London office he was going to insist Jo be the first one sent.

During the following week, the advent of a new love interest in Jason's life meant Brett was denied his most convenient refuge, and was forced to endure his misery alone. It might have been some compensation if his business life had been proceeding smoothly, but he couldn't even make that claim. The situation with the network hadn't improved any, and the owners of the chain of furniture stores he'd been sounding out so far hadn't shifted from their original indecisive interest.

In a desperate bid to assert control in at least one aspect of his life, he'd today upped his offer on the property he wanted by fifteen thousand dollars and managed to secure the deal. He didn't give a stuff that his lawyer was livid at him for acting without consulting him, or that he considered Brett insane for going so far over the market value. Brett figured it was the best fifteen grand he'd ever spent, since buying the house gave him a legitimate reason to celebrate. Which was exactly what he was going to do while Jo was out painting the town with Kyle, or Adam or whoever the devil was bound to turn up to collect her. And champagne *was* for celebrations, he told himself. If he'd just wanted to sit home and drown his sorrows he'd have bought a bottle of Scotch.

Setting his board against the back of the house, he slid open the back door and strode to the phone, daring it to stop ringing before he reached it.

'Hello,' he said, his jaw tightening with immediate tension at the caller's request. Not that it was a surprise these days to hear a male voice asking to speak to Joanna.

'She's not home yet,' he said, glancing at the clock and noting she was later than usual.

'Oh. That must be Brett, is it?'

He frowned, uneasy with the overt familiarity in a voice he didn't recognise. The caller didn't wait to have his question answered.

'It's Russell Burnswood, here, Brett. You're probably in the same position as me...' He chuckled. 'Know the name but not the face.'

Brett didn't know any such thing, but again the man gave him no time to say so.

'Listen, I've just found Joanna's wallet at my place, but I haven't been here since I dropped her back at the agency after lunch. Knowing Joanna, she'll be worried sick about where she left it, but if she's been ringing me to check she'll be none the wiser. She's expecting me at around seven tonight, but I didn't want her to worry unnecessarily...'

Even after he'd replaced the receiver Brett was still hearing the man's voice. More importantly, he was still hearing the obvious affection for Jo which had been behind the words, and a whole lot of other implications that had his blood boiling.

When she still wasn't home by six, as she was every Friday, he rang the agency. The phone was eventually answered by the cleaner, who curtly told Brett that as far as he knew he was the only person still in the building, and that he *wasn't* paid to keep track of the firm's staff. With his anger over Jo's mystery involvement with the unknown Russell Burnswood fast becoming intermingled with nagging concern at her unexplained absence, Brett came dangerously close to telling the man not to worry; Meaghan's wouldn't be paying him for *anything* in the future! Instead he grunted, 'Thanks for nothing, mate,' and slammed the receiver down.

Fifteen minutes later he literally sprinted to the front door when he heard a key click in the lock.

The initial blessed relief at seeing her unhurt vanished within seconds of her cheerful, 'Hi!'

'Where the hell have you been?' he demanded.

'I...I left my purse at—'

'I know where you left your damned purse,' he cut in. 'I want to know where you've been that you couldn't even bother to call!'

'I went back to Russell's to get it,' she told him, her voice hushed but terse. 'And I'm sorry if you were worried, but I've been trying to call you on the car phone for nearly an hour and getting a busy signal.'

'Car—' He stopped her attempt to close the door and stuck his head out in time to see a maroon Statesman complete a three-point turn and head off down the road. He spun back to glare at her. '*Whose* car phone?'

'Russell's.'

Brett was having a hard time collating things in his mind, but the departure of Russell definitely seemed like a good sign. Leaning back against the door, he allowed himself a smug grin. 'Guess the date is off, then, huh?'

Rubbing her forehead, as if completely exhausted with the discussion, she shook her head. 'Since we're running late he's going to get petrol while I shower and dress. So if you're through with the inquisition...'

Having his fledgling hopes battered put him back on the offensive. 'Sure!' he said, pushing away from the door. 'By all means go take your shower! But I suggest you give that cute little mouth of yours a good wash-out with soap too, princess! 'Cause I haven't been on the phone except for the few minutes it took to check and see if you were at work!'

Not trusting what might come out of his mouth next, he headed straight for the bar. He was on his second glass of Scotch when the doorbell chimed. Having seen the

Statesman swing into the drive, he remained in his chair. He was Jo's date; if she wanted to let him in she'd just have to answer the damned door in her robe!

Like hell!

CHAPTER SIXTEEN

BRETT'S anger was superseded by disbelief the moment he opened the front door. If this guy wasn't at least *five years* older than Brett himself was, then he must have had one hell of a tough life! Not that it showed in his trim athletic build, nor his well cut but uninspired navy suit, pinstriped shirt and old school tie. No, the evidence was in the flecks of grey at his temples and the weathered face, heavily grooved by what, to Brett, was a too friendly smile that radiated no warmth, nor reached his hard slate eyes.

Joanna was actually interested in this guy? He was so nonplussed by the possibility that it took the other man to instigate conversation.

'Russell Burnswood,' he said, thrusting out his right hand. 'You must be Brett. Joanna's mentioned you and your family so often I feel I know you already.'

Though his initial response to the handshake was purely automatic, Brett's brain checked back in a few seconds later and he stepped back to allow the man to enter.

Burnswood scanned the decor and the living room's eclectic mix of contemporary and period furnishing and dismissed it without comment.

'Have a seat,' Brett said, curious to see if he'd relax easily onto the sofa or perch uncomfortably on the edge of the antique wing-backed chair. He chose the chair, but with a blasé air suggestive of absolute confidence in himself.

'Joanna mentioned you were a television producer,' he said conversationally. 'I imagine you find it an interesting profession.'

'Not at the moment.'

For the life of him Brett couldn't see Jo laughing and

enthusing about candy floss with this guy. Despite the attempt at pally chit-chat, he wasn't the sort to put a person at ease. Then again, Brett conceded, his discomfort with the guy's presence could have had a lot to do with the fact jealousy had him itching to kick his miserable butt out through the front door. It took effort to even appear to be civil.

'I'm having a Scotch. Can I get you something?'

'Thank you. Water will be fine—don't drink alcohol myself.' He smiled. 'Always believed true enjoyment and relaxation can be drawn from within, without the need of artificial stimulants. One of the things I admire about Joanna,' he confided. 'Doesn't have any nasty habits.'

Fighting down the urge to say, *Guess she's never thrown up on your front lawn, huh?* Brett excused himself and went to fetch the requested drink. For the luxury of the few extra seconds it would keep him away from the jerk, he opted to go to the kitchen refrigerator rather than the one in the wet bar.

Where the devil had she met *this* guy? Not at any of the parties she'd told Brett about, that was for sure!

On his way back inside with the water he noticed the handpiece of the telephone was askew. It wasn't until he was replacing it that he recalled not only how he'd slammed it down when he'd last used it, but what he'd said to Jo when she'd said she'd been unable to get through.

'You bloody idiot!' he roared.

His first instinct was to rush inside and apologise to her, but then he realised that with Mr Excitement sitting in the wings waiting for her he probably wouldn't get a chance.

'*Damn!*'

'Problem, Brett?'

Turning, he found the man he'd left in the living room moving across the dining room, looking extremely concerned.

'Nothing I can't rectify.' *I hope!* 'Were you looking for something?' he asked pointedly.

'Oh, no. No, it's just when I heard your language I assumed the worst.'

'My apologies, Burnswood,' he said tightly, steering the man back to the living room, 'if I alarmed you.' Be damned if he'd say 'offended', because he didn't give a rat's backside about offending this pompous jerk!

'Oh, don't feel badly.'

Brett bit the inside of his mouth.

'While I don't swear myself, it's hard not to become somewhat immune to it in this day and age. Another of the reasons I find Joanna so delightful.' He paused and sipped his water. 'She's the essence of the contemporary yet with the values of the past. I know she's going to be a wonderful influence on my girls.'

'Your girls?'

'My daughters. Abigail, Bethany and Rachel. They've been becoming something of a handful since the two eldest hit their teens,' he said ruefully. 'Joanna's meeting them tonight, which is why I brought her back to change. Her get-up today was a tad too extreme, and unfortunately they're already wanting to wear the most appalling clothes. Still, I'm hoping they'll adore Joanna as much as I do. They do so need a woman's guidance, and who better than someone like her?'

'Your *wife*?' Brett suggested, knowing it was a vain hope even before the idiot shook his head.

'My wife walked out on her responsibilities before our eldest started school. Not that the girls haven't been better off for it. She was an utterly undesirable mother and the worst kind of wife. Wilful and rebellious.'

Though he'd never claimed to have psychic powers, the constriction in Brett's chest and gut told him he was spot on the money when it came to what was on this turkey's mind. Still, if he was going to strangle a man with his bare hands in the house, his mother would want to know he'd done it without a shadow of a doubt that it was justifiable.

Gripping his Scotch glass so hard he expected it to shatter, he forced himself to voice his gravest fear. 'Am I correct in assuming you're intending to ask Jo to *marry* you?'

Affirmation came in the man's egotistical grin. 'Not immediately, of course,' he said. 'She still has some rough edges which need smoothing, but nothing that isn't correctable.'

The cork coaster Brett's free hand was using as a worry bead snapped in two. *'Such as?'*

'Oh, minor things! Too much make-up…the skin-tight clothes. Nothing which isn't superficial. The important thing is Joanna has a kind heart and a genuine desire to please people. With patience, I think she could be made into the perfect wife; I doubt she's a selfish bone in her entire body.' He chuckled, then offered a conspiratorial wink. 'And you have to admit she has a *very* attractive body.'

Rage rolled through Brett's gut, but he set the Scotch glass down with infinite care and rose to his feet. 'Oh, I admit Jo's beautiful, inside and out. And I'm convinced she'd be the best wife a man could have,' he said. 'And you're absolutely right when you say she's not selfish. However…' Lunging forward, he grabbed Burnswood's lapels, hauling him to his feet amid the tinkle of glass splintering on the tiled floor.

'I *am* selfish, Burnswood! Which means if anyone's going to ruin her life by marrying her it's going to be *me*!'

The man's frantic struggles provided Brett with the pleasure of having to increase the force necessary to escort the mongrel to the front door. Then, concerned Burnswood's incoherent spluttering might bring Jo to investigate, he drew great satisfaction from gagging the protests by shoving the two halves of the coaster he still held into the gaping mouth and clamping a hand over it. *Hard!*

Instantly the irritating but ineffective blows to his ribs stopped as his opponent employed both hands to fight the one gagging him. Brett, however, needed the use of only one to open the front door, and while Burnswood was still bent over, trying simultaneously to suck air, spit cork and issue legal threats, he planted a foot squarely on the man's pompous backside and *shoved*!

Slamming the door shut, he pivoted and in eight strides was at the bathroom; it was silent and the door ajar. He pushed it wide…empty.

The peal of chimes began tinkling through the air.

Six more strides and he was outside her room; a buzz came from within and the door was closed. Unhesitatingly he turned the handle and flung it open.

With a gasp Jo's head came up from between her knees, her hair flying back and the humming dryer falling from her hands to the bed. Her face was flushed, those exotic almond eyes of hers wide with surprise and curiosity; her mouth formed a perfect glossy 'O'. Without doubt she was the most beautiful thing he'd ever seen, and he loved her so damned much he couldn't imagine how he was ever going to be able to put it into words.

Though she was only half dressed, in partially zipped jeans and a grey satin camisole that flowed like liquid silver with her slightest movement, she seemed more bemused by his presence than embarrassed.

'Brett…what's the matter?'

The sheer spellbinding beauty of her kept him speechless.

With innate grace she rose to her feet. 'Brett, what—?' She broke off, frowning. 'Is that the doorbell?'

'Probably.'

Reaching for the hairdryer, she switched it off. 'Brett, it *is* the doorbell.'

'So it is.' He closed the door.

'It…might be Russell back from—'

'It is Russell.' He advanced towards her with slow determined steps. 'But we're not letting him in.'

'We're not?'

'Nope. 'Cause I've just gone through the trouble of turfing him out.'

'Oh.'

There was a banked excitement in her eyes that increased both his pulse and his hopes as he halted in front of her. 'Do you want to know why?'

'Yes.' It was barely a whisper.

'Because,' he said, 'I can't think of one reason why I'm continuing to drive myself insane trying to keep my hands off you, when you're dating a jerk who's even older than I am.'

Her head dipped at the words. A heartbeat later it came back up; the tears in her eyes brought an instant crippling pain, momentarily robbing him of the ability to recognise the shy, uncertain smile hovering at her mouth.

'Is it any consolation to know it's been driving me insane too?'

He had no idea who moved first, but once she was in his arms and he could hold her, kiss her, it didn't matter. Nothing mattered except knowing that moment carried the same wonder, bliss and overwhelming relief for her as it did for him.

Trusting her arms to keep her body tight against his, he clamped his hands on her face to rain kisses over every molecule of her flawless skin and each incredibly gorgeous feature. Her perfectly arched jet eyebrows, the delicate lids of those eyes which had stopped him in his tracks the first day he met her, and her nose, which was as elegant yet unpretentious as she herself. Only then did he return to pay homage to the sweet, sensual mouth that created smiles which captivated his heart and revealed a joyful spirit which had refreshed his jaded soul.

Over and over again he worshipped with his lips the face of this woman whose beauty encompassed so much more than the mere physical that it had driven him beyond reason. *And he had been beyond reason.* Until today. Until a fool had sacrilegiously claimed this woman needed changing. Only a fool would mess with perfection. And only a far bigger fool would willingly surrender it to another. The recollection of how seriously he'd contemplated disregarding the strength of his feelings for Joanna drove him to deepen his kiss in the search for yet more assurances that this moment exceeding even his wildest imaginings was in fact reality.

The sensations created by her eager response to the insistent demands of his tongue had his heart bursting with love and tenderness, yet simultaneously they provoked a panicked desire to touch and explore every part of her. It was a desire both eased and fed by her hands' frantic movements up his chest, across his shoulders and back.

It was some time before the initial frenetic excitement of finally being able to release his deepest feelings abated sufficiently to allow Brett to try and verbalise them in semi-coherent speech as they stood hugging each other in limp breathlessness.

'Oh, Lord, Jo…' The words were a prayer. A plea. A substitute for all the things he wanted to say, but which he couldn't hope to articulate in the short span of a lifetime. It hardly seemed enough to have just said he loved—

His thoughts skidded to a halt. Frowning, he tried to recall if he had actually *told* her how he felt somewhere amid the jumbled semi-articulate words he'd uttered in his haste to physically express himself. He supposed it hardly mattered, for it was evident that she knew exactly how he felt from the way she was nestled against him. Yet for some reason he wanted to hear himself say the words.

Smiling, he placed a finger under her chin to lift her head from where it rested against his heart. 'In case you haven't noticed…I'm crazy in love with you, Joanna Ford.'

She lifted a hand to gently run her knuckles along his jaw, and he felt fire ignite down his spine. 'I think I fell in love with you, Brett McAlpine, within the first minute of seeing you.'

'Gotta query that,' he said, bending so his mouth could nibble on the silky skin of her neck. 'You thought I was gay.'

'Not right away. Not until I mentioned to Karessa about moving out. And the only reason I did that was because you made me feel so…'

'So what?' he prompted.

'Sooo…' A shiver of delight went through her as, watching her intently, he slid the camisole straps from her shoulders. *'Aware.'*

'Aware of what?' he teased, earning an amused glare.

'You know what…*you*!' A tinge of pink rose on her cheeks and she lowered her eyes to where her fingers were playing speculatively with his top button. 'You were the most fascinating man I'd ever met. At first it was a relief to think you were gay, because I knew you'd never be interested in me. I thought that would make my attraction fade, but it didn't, and I started to think there was something wrong with me, and I was so terrified I'd embarrass you, and—and…'

He tilted her head back, so she was looking at him. 'Oh, sweetheart…I *was* interested.' He smiled, grazing his thumbs over her cheekbones. 'I walked into that foyer, instantly drowned in these incredible eyes, and a second later I had you mentally stripped down to nothing but those damn sexy boots you were wearing.' His fingers felt the heat of her flush. 'I mightn't have known then that I'd already fallen in love with you, but I sure as hell knew I wanted to fall into bed with you.'

There was genuine feminine pleasure in her shy smile. 'And…do you still want to…' She paused and nibbled her lip, but her gaze didn't waver from his. 'Um…fall into bed with me?'

'No… Now I want to make love to you. There's a difference.' Both his body and heart tightened at the flare of desire that sparked in her eyes.

'I…I didn't know that.'

'That's because I'm the only man in the world who'll ever love you enough to show it to you.'

She smiled. 'Will you show me now?'

Choking on too many emotions to frame an answer, he tumbled them onto the bed and let his mouth respond with wordless affirmation. An affirmation that commenced with a thorough exploration of her mouth and engaged her agile, eager tongue in a duel which on its own had him rock-hard and threatened his control. To avoid being wiped out by the tidal wave of passion building within him, he turned his attention to the creamy smoothness of her neck. But she arched against him, and the need to feel and see all of her created havoc with his best intentions. But then from day one his best intentions had done nothing but keep him on a road to hell, and—

'Ah, hell,' he muttered, pulling back from her. 'Honey, we need to talk.'

She blinked. *'Now?'*

'Yeah,' he said, irritated as hell at his timing. 'The thing is, Jo, I'm crazy about you. I love you more than I even imagined it was possible to love someone. And I want to marry you.'

'Oh, Brett, I—'

'Shh. Don't answer until I explain everything. I know you're only twenty-two, but I swear I'm not going to hold you from your dreams. I'm happy to wait ten years if you want to, to have kids. And as soon as you get a passport I'll take you anywhere in the world you want to go. We can take a year off now and go overseas, and then travel four months of every year after that. We'll go anywhere you like and do whatever you want,' he vowed. 'But, honey…I need to know you really believe I can make you happy before I make love to you…because once I do I'm never going to be able to walk away from you.'

'Oh, Brett!' She launched herself at him with such force he ended up on his back. Her kiss was long and lingering, and when she pulled back she was smiling as tears seeped from her eyes.

'I don't need all those trips to make me happy. I just need you.'

'But you want to travel,' he insisted. 'You've always said that it was your dream.'

'Only because I couldn't ever imagine someone I loved would love me back. Travel just seemed a more attainable source of happiness to me. Brett, you've already fulfilled my most exotic dream. I don't need a passport…I just need you.

As his heart began to well with the most glorious joy, she took his face firmly between her hands.

'So, yes, you can make me happy.' She kissed him. 'Yes, I'll marry you.' She kissed him again. 'But, no, I won't wait ten years to make babies with you. I know what it's like to have old parents and I don't want that for our children.'

The way she said 'our children' spread a liquid heat through Brett's loins, and this time when she kissed him he locked a hand on the back of her head to stop her withdrawing and engaged her in something more sensory than words.

'If you're all through talking now,' he teased, 'there's a man here who really wants to make love to you.'

Those magic eyes of hers dilated with desire. 'That's good,' she said, lowering her head with a look that was pure seduction. 'Because I've dreamed about him doing it…' She paused at the last minute so that her lips brushed his as she spoke. 'Oh, and by the way, I'm not twenty-two. I'm twenty-four.'

Then her mouth opened over his and her hands slipped beneath his shirt and Brett forgot every thought he'd ever had. The lazy exploration of her hands against his flesh inspired his own to seek similar pleasures, and he tugged the satin camisole to her armpits before rolling her onto her back so he could savour the view as her breasts were exposed.

He only managed a groan of awe before he was compelled to draw one of the cherry peaks into his mouth and relish its pebbled hardness against his tongue. Her throaty moan as she arched closer to his mouth inspired him to transfer his attention to the other, before nuzzling the valley between them. With her hands in his hair and the whimpering sound of her growing arousal ringing in his ears he blazed a trail of hot, hungry kisses across and down her abdomen, until the open zipper of her jeans scratched against his cheek to remind him that clothing still hampered his intention to worship every centimetre of her skin.

Shrugging free of his shirt, he stood and proceeded to dispose of his trousers and boxers in one effort.

'Y-you're beautiful,' she whispered, and pride almost brought him to his knees.

'And you,' he said, gently taking the camisole over her head and then placing his hands on the denim riding low on her hips, 'are exquisite.'

Yet even as he'd said the words he hadn't been prepared for the almost spiritual impact of her nude perfection, and it was necessary to close his eyes and regather his control before he again trusted himself to rejoin her on the bed. When he did, he once more sought her mouth and feasted upon her sweetness for gloriously long minutes before starting a secondary oral excursion down her body. Her startled gasp of air as he nuzzled the jet down at the junction of her thighs gave him pause, so, too, did the sight of the knuckle-white grip her hands had on the bedding. Reaching for her hands, he closed his own over them, and as he met those magnificent thick-lashed eyes they were *all* the colours of love and trust.

'Love me…' she urged, turning her hands beneath his and linking their fingers. 'Love me as no one else has ever or will ever love me.'

And he did. He felt and tasted her fly apart in her passion. He heard her chanting his name at her moment of release. And when his own could no longer be denied he rose above her, and as their gazes met he claimed her for always and fulfilled his own dreams.

EPILOGUE

THEY married six weeks later, necessitating an early return from Europe for Brett's mother, who really didn't mind in the slightest and proclaimed she thought Joanna showed real flair for interior design. It also required a hastily created wedding dress by Carlo, who minded a great deal because 'true genius cannota be rushed!'

Jason was, of course, flattered to be asked to be best man, and even more flattered by the charming Steve Cooper, who gave Joanna away.

Karessa was thrilled at being a bridesmaid, and requested that as her bridesmaid gift she'd like Brett and Joanna to bring her something back from their honeymoon in Germany; preferably a tall, blond ski-instructor.

And Meaghan, who'd decided the London deal wasn't a goer after all, continued to swear black and blue that she'd made an honest mistake about Joanna's age and asked if Brett was planning on getting off her case any time before Joanna's fiftieth birthday. Brett said no.

For their first anniversary Joanna saw Scandinavia.

For their second Brett took her to Disneyland.

For their third they conceived their first child in Paris, and fittingly named her...Paris.

For their fourth anniversary, Joanna flatly refused to go anywhere outside of a hundred-kilometre radius of her three-month-old daughter, because she'd recently read an article that advised against separating mother and child in the first year. So Brett secretly booked an airline ticket and a Sydney hotel room and took her to see a sister who was desperate to be forgiven and experience the spiritual love of real family...

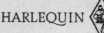

MEN at WORK

All work and no play?
Not these men!

July 1998
MACKENZIE'S LADY by Dallas Schulze
Undercover agent Mackenzie Donahue's
lazy smile and deep blue eyes were his best
weapons. But after rescuing—and kissing!—
damsel in distress Holly Reynolds, how could
he betray her by spying on her brother?

August 1998
MISS LIZ'S PASSION by Sherryl Woods
Todd Lewis could put up a building with ease,
but quailed at the sight of a classroom! Still,
Liz Gentry, his son's teacher, was no battle-ax,
and soon Todd started planning some
extracurricular activities of his own....

September 1998
A CLASSIC ENCOUNTER
by Emilie Richards
Doctor Chris Matthews was intelligent, sexy
and *very* good with his hands—which made
him all the more dangerous to single mom
Lizette St. Hilaire. So how long could she
resist Chris's special brand of TLC?

Available at your favorite retail outlet!

MEN AT WORK™

 HARLEQUIN®  Silhouette®

Look us up on-line at: http://www.romance.net   PMAW2

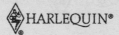

Not The Same Old Story!

Exciting, glamorous romance stories that take readers around the world.

Harlequin Romance
Sparkling, fresh and tender love stories that bring you pure romance.

HARLEQUIN
Temptation
Bold and adventurous— Temptation is strong women, bad boys, great sex!

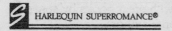
Provocative and realistic stories that celebrate life and love.

Contemporary fairy tales—where anything is possible and where dreams come true.

HARLEQUIN
INTRIGUE®
Heart-stopping, suspenseful adventures that combine the best of romance and mystery.

Humorous and romantic stories that capture the lighter side of love.